Aesop Revisited:

Ancient Lessons with a Biblical Perspective

Aesop Revisited: Ancient Lessons with a Biblical Perspective, by Eugene M. Slavit,

Published by Evangelist Publications.

All rights reserved.

Cover art and design: Gene Slavit

All illustrations: Gene Slavit

Printing year 2019. Revised 2021

All scriptures and stories based on scriptures are taken from the Authorized King James Version of the Bible.

To Eli Max & Ruth Slavit

and to

William & Barbara Simmons,

For raising me and Sherry

With love and kindness.

Preface

One of the treasures that my wife received from her father was a copy of *Fables of Aesop* (copyright 1925, by Albert Whitman & Company). The text was based on the works of Jean de La Fontaine (France) and Samuel Croxall (England). I loved reading the simple and terse text along with more than seventy colored illustrations by Joseph E. Dash. This illustrator had a good feel for how animals acted, and included phrasing from the text for each illustration. I have often read this book to our son in his youth and continue to glean treasures of wisdom from it.

My elementary and high school years were filled with visits to our local library where I spent hours devouring ancient Greek mythology, American Tall Tales, Norse legend, and other international folk tales. I remember spending many a summer during my teens in our family's living-room reclining chair as I reread some of my favorite myths. This love continued into my university days where I received a bachelor's degree in Classical Studies.

About forty-five years ago, I purposefully accepted Jesus Christ as lord and believed that God raised him from the dead. Being raised a Roman Catholic, I was exposed to these ideas from my youth and may have inadvertently been saved at an earlier age. But during my searching period at the age of twenty, I knew for certain that I was born again of God's spirit. As I studied the Bible, I found that it was indeed God's Word with all things that pertain to life and godliness. I am aware of the Christ-based origin of most heroic stories, especially those still seen in the heavens by their original constellation names. Recently while reading *Fables of Aesop*, I was struck by the similarity of Aesop's morals with the truths in the Book of Proverbs. I also realized how similar the fables were to records of men and women in the Bible. The animal genre is quite simple to understand in Aesop, and the same principles of living can be recognized in the lives of those described in Biblical records.

Thus I began a three-month period of writing *Aesop Revisited: Ancient Lessons with a Biblical Perspective*. My method was to think of someone in the Bible who matched the lesson exhibited by the fox or wolf or lion or dog in Aesop, and then to use the same brief style to get the same lesson across. Having been a bit of a sketcher since my youth, I added illustrations to match the Biblical record. I trust that this work will prove valuable to those who love both a good story, and an encapsulation of truth.

Eugene M. Slavit
Rancho Palos Verdes,
September 24, 2019

I have enhanced the illustrations digitally and enlarged them in many cases. The text remains the same. The quotation for each illustration is now in the body of the text and set in boldface colored font. Although this volume has changed, God's grace and goodness in Christ has not. Happy reading. – Eugene M. Slavit (2021)

Introduction

The stories in this volume are set in the same order and with the exact same "morals" as in *Fables of Aesop* (copyright 1925, by Albert Whitman & Company), based on the works of Jean de La Fontaine (France) and Samuel Croxall (England). Each has been rewritten using a Biblical example. Some Bible stories are repeated when they can be used to teach a different moral. Many Biblical records are not mentioned at all. Of course, the most commonly noted characters are Jesus Christ, his apostles, Pharisees, Moses, Samuel, Saul, and David. Many stories come from the historical records in the Bible books of Judges, Samuel, Kings, and Chronicles. Specific stories like Esther, Daniel and his friends, Nehemiah, and Joshua are also used in the narrative.

The content of the stories ranges from innocent subjects to more mature themes like greed, pride, sexual immorality, murder, and hatred. Many Bible stories, especially from the Old Testament, are violent in nature—but carry important lessons on real-life problems. This book can be used for small children, but some stories may be too difficult for their tender hearts. Most stories are appropriate for teens and adults of all ages.

The illustrations are added to give a "feel" for the events described in each story. They are not designed to be factual or an exact representation of the Biblical narrative. Hopefully, they will add perspective to each story and help them become more "alive" to the reader. Each illustration is based on a **text from the story (set in this boldface color style)** that gives an important lesson to be learned.

Since so many of these "morals" are similar to the maxims found in the Book of Proverbs, an appendix is added to show similarities between these two literary works. All quotations are taken from the King James Version of the Bible. Many of the Proverbs were written by Solomon, the son of David and ruler of the united kingdom of Judah and Israel. His life is well documented both in the Bible and secular history. But who was the author of the more than one-hundred Fables in this book?

During my studies to acquire a degree in Classical Studies, I spent hours in the original Greek and Latin works of ancient authors. Aesop was a Greek. Aristotle (a Greek writer from the 4th century B.C.) says that Aesop was born around 600 B.C. in the vicinity of Thrace. Phaedrus (a Roman writer from the first century A.D.) said Aesop was born in Phrygia, or modern Turkey. The great Greek historian Herodotus (5th century B.C.) gives a biography of Aesop: a slave in Samos, later freed, and meeting an untimely end in Delphi. Plutarch confirmed this incident six centuries later, adding that Aesop was falsely accused of temple theft and then thrown off a cliff by the Delphians.

Whatever the details of Aesop's life, his work is a masterpiece. A collection of Aesop's fables was put together by Demetrius of Phalerum in the third century B.C., amounting to ten volumes. Phaedrus (noted above) translated the fables into Latin, as did his Syrian contemporary Babrius, putting them into poetic verse. Since that time, the fables of Aesop have had many stories added from other cultures. Jean de La Fontaine and Samuel Croxall are only two of many who developed this "animal story" genre to point out human foibles and virtues.

Finally, let me remind the reader that this volume is unique in that it points out age-old morals by using the fountainhead of truth—the Bible. It is my firm conviction that all in the Bible is true, even if misunderstood or mistranslated from the original revelation given. It may take the reader a diligent effort to gain a scope and understanding of the scriptures, but the labor is well worth the joy of an intimate relationship with the Father. May this volume add to that understanding and joy.

Table of Contents

Dedication 3
Preface 4
Introduction 5
The Boy and His Brothers 8
The Killer and His Victim 9
The General and
the Greedy Soldier 10
The Would-be Friend 11
The Woman and the Serpent 12
The People and Their King 13
The Deceiving Relatives 14
The Prince and His Father 15
The Two Kings 16
The Runaway Slave 17
The Murderous King 18
The Fatal Assembly 19
The Faithless Follower 20
The Foolish Nephew 21
The Successful Suitor 22
The Conquered Hero 23
The Renegade's Army 24
The Left-handed Savior 25
The Jealous Brothers 26
The Wise Leader 27
The Queen's Dear Cousin 28
The Good Young Man 30
The Disguised Queen 32
The True Mother 33
A Selfish People 34
The Four Captives 35
The Lying Escapee 36
The Shameful Calf 37
The "Clever" General 38
The Lustful Prince
and His False Friend 39
A Turn of Events 41
The Ungrateful Landowner 42
The Unfaithful Guests 43
The Blind Man
and the Prophet 44
The Corrupted Seer 45
Lesson from a Gourd 46
The Four Young Rebels 47
The Courageous Innkeeper 48
A Narrow Escape 49
The Slain Giant 50
The Flattering Prince 51

The Resentful Captain 52
The Foolhardy Twin 53
The Dishonest
Father-in-law 54
The Unthankful People 55
The Unfaithful Relatives 56
The Besieged City 57
The Complaining Travelers 58
The Noble Exile 59
The Treacherous King
and His Family 60
The Disobedient Ruler 61
The Wise Judge 62
The Cowardly Spies 63
The Proud and
Foolish Ruler 64
The Murderous Ruler
and the Astronomers 65
Worthless Wealth 66
The King and His Captive 67
The Presumptuous Servant 68
The Disrespectful Youths 69
The Dissatisfied Ruler 70
The False "Prophet" 71
The Foolish Twin 72
The Talking Donkey 73
The Widow's Story 74
The "Mad" General 75
The Well-loved Soldier 76
The Lying General 77
The Waylaid Kings 78
The Evil Sorceress 79
The Wise Prophet
and His Foes 80
The Obstinate Ruler 81
The Hapless Suitor 82
The Harsh and Haughty
Young Ruler 83
The Murderous Messenger 84
The Woman at the
Ancient Well 85
The Mysterious Message 86
The False "Father's Son" 87
The Persistent Hitman 88
The Heroic Captain's Vow 89
The Prideful Prince 90
The Hopeful Assassins 91

The Amazed Deputy 92
Persistent Evil 93
The Tyrant's Excuses 94
The Over-confident
Prince 95
The Foolish Savior 96
The Curser's Reward 97
The Duplicitous Prophet 98
The Oracles' Advice 99
The Ambitious Servant 101
The Pleasure-seeking King
and His Noble Captain 102
The Teacher and
the Hypocrites 104
The King and the
Necromancer 105
The Conceited Leader 106
The One-week Ruler 107
The Notorious Prophet 108
The Treacherous
General 109
The Evil King's Advice 110
The Honest Prophet 111
The Longsuffering Uncle 112
The King's Servant 113
The Promoted Youth 114
The Childless Queen 115
The Outspoken Leader 116
The Hidden Prophet 117
The Fear-filled King 118
The Courageous Savior 119
The Wise Woman 120
The Kangaroo Court 121
The Uncivil Ruler 122
The Sorcerer's
Repentance 123
The King's Burdens 124
The Enlightened
Apprentice 125
The Clever Captive 126
The Vain Bewitcher 127
The Lying Thief 128
The Foolishly Greedy
Rich Man 129
The Crushed Conqueror 130
Appendix—Proverbs 131
About the Author 167

> **The Boy and His Brothers**
> **("The Hare and the Tortoise"** in light of I Samuel 8—16)

The people of a faraway land desired to have a king like the realms around them. Before this time, they had been guided by an elderly and kindly prophet. The prophet argued that no king was needed if they would follow divine guidance, but the people were obstinate. The man selected to be king was very tall and very strong. But he proved to be weak in character and spiritual insight. Thus, a new king was needed and the prophet was sent to find him. Being directed to the countryside, he came upon a man with seven sons. The prophet knew that the new king would be one of these sons. When he saw the oldest son, the prophet said to himself, **"Surely this is the new king. He is the biggest and strongest."**

But the divine guidance was not so. The prophet then looked at five more sons. None of them would do. Finally, he asked the father if he had any more children. The man said, "Just one, the youngest, and he is out with the sheep." The prophet had the boy brought to him, and he knew that this lad was to be the new king. His divine guidance was: "People look at the outward appearance, but you should look on the heart."

***** *"Biggest is not always best."* *****

> **The Killer and His Victim**
> **("The Lion and the Mouse** in light of Acts 9:1-18)

A vicious and politically powerful man so hated his religious enemies that he made it his duty to find, imprison, and often kill them. Once, while traveling to a distant city to carry out his evil intent, he was struck from his horse by a bright light. **Being blinded, he was led into the city and left alone.**

One of this man's intended victims, someone of little worldly "importance," learned of his enemy's plight and sought him out. His divine guidance was to put his hands upon the blind man's eyes, and he was healed. Thus, this man of great renown was set free by one of little acclaim, and his avowed enemy at that.

***** *"Little friends may prove great friends."* *****

> **The General and the Greedy Soldier**
> **("The Goose with the Golden Eggs"** in light of Joshua 6 & 7**)**

A valiant general led his army to victory and conquered a mighty city, with its very walls crashing before them. He adjured his troops to take no booty from this forsaken fortress lest they bring reproach upon their people and curse their future campaigns. **But one soldier was entranced by a beautifully-woven robe, piles of silver coins, and a wedge of gold.**

He rejoined the general for the next battle, and things went awry for this previously undefeated army. The inhabitants of a much smaller city chased them and slew them in their tracks. The general was dumbfounded and wondered why they had been so handily beaten. Then he realized that a curse was upon his people. He gathered the tribes together and discovered who had taken forbidden spoil. The general took the greedy and disobedient soldier with the robe and silver and gold, along with his sons and daughters and all his livestock—and killed them all. Thus was the curse removed and the army returned to a march of victory. For as the general said, "You have troubled us, and so you and all you have will be troubled this day!"

***** *"Greed often costs more than one could imagine."* *****

> **The Would-be Friend**
> **("The Two Pots"** in light of II Chronicles 22:1-9 & II Kings 9:14-29)

Once, a king married an evil witch, who beguiled him with her sorcery. She bore him a son, who grew to be king in his father's stead, while she became the dowager queen. The ruler of a neighboring country joined in a military alliance with the king, and **they went out in company together to battle the king's enemies.**

The king was wounded and returned to be healed, and his friend, the ruler, joined him there. At this time, there arose a mighty and valiant warrior who was tasked with removing the evil influences of the witch. He learned that her son, the king, was recuperating and drove his chariot furiously to the city where he lay. After quickly dispatching the king with an arrow straight through his heart, the warrior then turned upon the ruler who had recently befriended the king. Thus the ruler of a fair land lost his life for associating with the son of so vile a creature as the witch.

***** *"Be careful of the company you keep."* *****

> ### The Woman and the Serpent
> ### ("The Fox and the Crow" in light of Genesis 3:1-6)

Abrilliant and powerful angel became so vain that he thought himself to be greater than his Creator. Thus he fell from the light and became the author of evil and lies. Taking the form of a serpent, he approached the first woman. For he knew the Creator had given her and her husband great power and authority over the world around them—and he wished to have that power for himself.

Engaging the woman in conversation, the serpent told her that since she was so magnificent, she could even rival her Creator in wisdom and knowledge. Falling for his flattery, she disobeyed the Creator and also encouraged her husband to do the same. Thus, they surrendered their authority to the serpent, who handily began to mock them and use that very power against them.

*****"The flatterer robs by stealth,
taking from his victim both wisdom and wealth."*****

> ### The People, the Judge, and Their King
> ### ("Jupiter and the Ass" in light of I Samuel 8)

A simple and nomadic people had been shepherded for years by "judges," who delivered them from their enemies and showed them how to live. A benevolent judge had two sons who were very evil and abused the people. The people were not content to accept their lot, but hoped for something better. So they demanded that the judge give them a king, such as they had seen in neighboring lands. **This angered the judge, but he was guided to give in to their foolish request.**

He warned them that a king would take advantage of them—forcing them and their children to serve in menial tasks and taking their goods for his own use. The people paid this no mind and clamored to be ruled. The wise judge's words came to pass, for the new king was a vain and reckless leader who greatly endangered the people. Thus the people's plight was far worse than if they had been content to be guided by the benevolent judge.

***** *"Contentment is the first law of happiness."* *****

> **The Deceiving Relatives**
> **("The Hawk and the Nightingale" in light of Deuteronomy 13:6-11)**

There once was a tribe led by a powerful and wise prophet who gave the people commandments and laws for their good. It so happened that evil spiritual forces tried to seduce some of the people so that these spirits could be worshipped by them. The prince of these evil spirits even used the natural affection of husbands for wives, wives for husbands, parents for children, and of close companions for each other to beguile them into this false worship. The prophet commanded that these deceiving relatives should be put to death if they refused to stop their ruinous behavior.

Yet a father or mother might say to themselves, "This is my son, I cannot see him killed. I would spare him." The prophet knowing this, straightly commanded that those who were the most intimate with the offenders were to be the first to stop this evil by killing the offender. They were not to wait for another day, but act swiftly and surely.

***** *"A little correct action today is worth countless attempts at righting things in the future."* *****

➢ **The Prince and His Father**
  ("The Traveler and His Dog" in light of I Samuel 14**)**

A faithless and selfish king grew afraid of the kingdoms around him. He despondently loitered under a pomegranate tree in luxury while his subjects waited for him to lead them to victory over their enemies. Then one day while the king delayed, his courageous son advanced with his armor-bearer upon the enemy and single-handedly defeated a great force. The king, being very religious, had told his people not to eat of any spoil, and thus their hunger weakened and limited their ability to fight. Yet the prince led them to victory, and many who were hiding in caves came forth to join the fray. The prince and the people found much wild honey in the forest, but the people refrained from eating any because of the king's command.

The prince, unaware of his father's rash and stupid edict, gladly partook of the honey and was strengthened to fight more valiantly. This religious king tried to kill his own son for breaking his "law," but the people refused to allow him to do such evil. The king prized himself as a great leader that all should follow, but in reality, it was the prince who was ready for action and the true hero of the day.

***** *"The loiterer often imputes delay to his more active friend."* *****

> ## The Two Kings
> ### ("The Cat and the Fox" in light of I Kings 22:1-38 & II Chronicles 18)

A noble king visited his evil and idolatrous fellow monarch. When asked to join his neighbor in battling for an ancient city, the visiting king agreed. Yet it was his habit to seek divine counsel before proceeding. Heeding his request, his idolatrous neighbor reluctantly called in a true and honest prophet, who denounced such a military expedition.

Nonetheless, both kings proceeded together—the noble king dressed in his full royal garments, and the evil king disguised as a common soldier. In the heat of battle, the noble king was surrounded by enemy forces, for they thought, because of the robes he wore, that he was the idolatrous king. At that point, the noble king cried out for divine protection. His prayer was answered, for the enemy forces recognized that this was not the king they sought and turned from him (since their ruler had instructed them to kill no other person in battle than the evil king).

On the other hand, the idolatrous king, who trusted in his disguise to save him, was wounded and killed by an arrow that "on chance" pierced a small slit in his armor. Thus his many feints and plans of deception were of no avail, while his neighbor's heartfelt prayer proved to be the safe way that brought deliverance even against the greatest odds.

***** *"Better one safe way than a hundred on which you cannot depend."* *****

> **The Runaway Slave**
> **("The Dove and the Ant"** in light of the Book of Philemon**)**

A slave escaped from his master and, travelling to a faraway city, was captured and imprisoned. There he met an elderly prisoner, and often comforted him and refreshed this old man in chains. It so happened that this elder prisoner had mightily helped the slave's former master in time past, who therefore owed the old man a great debt.

Upon learning of such a coincidence, the ancient prisoner wrote to the master, beseeching him to take back his slave without punishment (for a runaway slave faces death for his crime). Thus the slave's good deeds did not go unrewarded, and the elderly prisoner thankfully passed on a blessing to his new-found friend.

***** *"One good turn deserves another."* *****

> ### The Murderous King
> #### ("The Fox and the Mask" in light of Matthew 14:1-12 & Mark 6:14-29)

An emperor took the widow of his brother to wife, which action was promptly condemned by a wandering prophet. Thus, the empress sought an occasion to slay the prophet for his forthright proclamation.

One day the emperor, decked in royal attire, gave a lavish birthday feast for himself, complete with rich delicacies and entertainment. Prompted by her mother, the empress's daughter danced for her stepfather the emperor, and he was entranced beyond measure. Her performance so pleased him and his guests that he cried out in rapture, "I will give thee whatsoever thou wilt, even unto half of my kingdom!"

Seizing upon this opportunity, the empress induced her daughter to ask for the prophet's head—and though it saddened the emperor, he was forced to keep his public oath. Thus the prophet was quickly and mercilessly slain, and the richly-adorned king proved by his vicious deeds that he himself was inwardly of little worth.

***** *"Outside show is a poor substitute for inner worth."* *****

> **The Fatal Assembly**
> (**"The Wood and the Clown"** in light of II Kings 10:18-27)

Wishing to rid the land of image-grove worship, a zealous and decisive warrior set up a snare for such worshippers. After slaying their idolatrous king, he said, **"Your former master served the images a little, I will serve them much!"**

So he called all the prophets of the groves to meet with him, under penalty of death for refusing to come. The warrior commanded them to proclaim a special assembly of the worshippers—and every one of them came, so that the house of images was filled with people from one end to the other. After handing out special garments to them, the crowd was searched to see that no worshipper was missing, and that no non-worshippers were present. The warrior surrounded the house with his soldiers, straightly ordering them to soon kill everyone inside (for if any escaped, that soldier would pay with his own life).

Once the image ceremony was finished and all present had shown their allegiance, the soldiers entered and slew all, not a soul was missed. Only as they took their last breaths did the image worshippers realize that they had foolishly given their devotion to a profitless cause, and their supposedly new "champion" was their greatest nemesis.

***** *"To give well one must give wisely."* *****

> ## The Faithless Follower
> ("The Travelers and the Bear" in light of Matthew 26:14,47; Mark 14:10,43; Luke 22:3,47 & John 13:27; 18:3)

There once was a mighty prophet who traveled about and gathered unto himself a small band of followers. These men lived with their master and saw his many powerful deeds.

One of them was entrusted with the finances of the group, and was also given special recognition and an honored seat at their meal.

But when danger approached the group, that follower not only ran away, but also assisted the tormentors in capturing the prophet. Even though the prophet later rose from the dead and forgave the follower, this unfaithful man proved untrustworthy, never serving his master again.

***** *"Never trust a friend who deserts you in time of need."* *****

> **The Foolish Nephew**
> ("The Lion and the Four Oxen" in light of Genesis 12, 13, 19 & II Peter 2:7,8)

A wise and prosperous man brought his beautiful wife and his nephew to a new land of his dreams. After a famine came upon them there, they moved to a magnificent empire where the man's wit and his wife's beauty brought them even greater wealth. Leaving there, they returned to the "dream home" and found vast lands where they could raise their livestock. They were happy and stood united with the nephew against their common enemies, and thus saw protection and increase.

But one day the man's herdsmen and those of his nephew began to argue over their pastures. **This grew to such an intense rivalry that they parted asunder, with the nephew moving to what seemed to be the finest of the land—but was in reality near a city filled with wicked and evil men.**

Without his uncle's wisdom and protection, he was soon embroiled in war with his neighbors and taken captive, only to be rescued by his valiant uncle.

Rather than rejoining the safety and strength of his uncle's home, the nephew remained in this wicked city which was soon to be destroyed. Learning of his nephew's impending demise, the uncle prayed and the nephew was rescued by supernatural forces. Yet the nephew suffered for his divisiveness, losing his wife and seeing great reproach upon his children and their heirs.

***** *"United we stand, divided we fall."* *****

> ### The Successful Suitor
> #### ("The Fox and the Goat" in light of I Samuel 18:17-30)

A king had gained much of his wealth and power with the help of a young and valiant general. But the king grew jealous and fearful of the general's youth and success. He rashly hatched a plot to rid himself of his supposed rival. Offering his daughter to be the general's bride, he requested a dowry of one hundred tokens from the slain bodies of their enemy.

Thinking that this attempt would bring the general to certain death, the king was shocked when the general returned with double the amount requested. Thus the king, by his lack of foresight, enhanced the prestige and power of the one he feared.

***** *"Look before you leap."* *****

> **The Conquered Hero**
> **("The Bald Man and the Fly"** in light of Judges 16**)**

An invincible fighter drew his strength from a divine oath he had made in his youth. This gave him superhuman strength so that he heroically killed thousands of his enemies and pulled down their strongholds. Since they could not defeat him with brute force, his enemies conspired to entice him into handing over the secret to his power.

Bribing a beautiful harlot, they waited in her apartment to capture the fighter there in the event they could learn the source of his strength. She seductively asked him time and again where his might came from, but he used trickery to confuse her and those lying in wait. Yet his constant notice of her charms finally became his undoing. Being worn down by her constant entreaties, he revealed the truth about his oath.

At that point, his despicable enemies rushed in to bind him and then mocked him before all. He learned too late that it is better to have nothing to do with agents of evil.

***** *"You will only injure yourself if you take notice of despicable enemies."* *****

23

> **The Renegade's Army**
> **("The Crow and the Pitcher"** in light of I Chronicles 12:1-22)

A faithful and honest soldier was hated and hounded by an evil and jealous ruler. His former master would seek him in highways and byways, caves and gullies, mountains and plains. On many an occasion the soldier escaped imminent death with his few close friends.

As news of this unjust persecution reached the ears of other honest soldiers, they left the evil ruler and joined forces with their renegade compatriot in the wilderness. **These were no ordinary men—they were mighty, battle-ready, and capable with any weapon. Their faces were courageous and formidable as a lion; they were as agile and swift as a mountain gazelle.**

When the outlawed soldier saw them approach, he met them with exercised caution, in case this was a trap set by his former master. They met his challenge with a pure-hearted declaration: "We are yours and on your side! Peace be to you and to all your helpers, for you have divine support in all you do." Thus day by day, little by little, more and more defected from the evil king to the side of this honest soldier, until they were a mighty host.

***** *"Little by little does the trick."* *****

> **The Left-handed Savior**
> **("The Brother and Sister"** in light of Judges 3:12-30)

For eighteen years, a once-noble people were oppressed and subjugated by a neighboring ruler. There was among this people a man who was left-handed, which in their culture was considered ugly and odd. Nonetheless, he used his wits to fashion a two-sided dagger and hid it upon his right thigh—where none of the ruler's men would likely check, and where he could grab it with his good hand.

Thus prepared, he brought a gift to the ruler on behalf of his people, who summarily dismissed him along with all the other sycophants and vassals after receiving their tribute. But the left-hander again used his wits and returned unto the ruler, whispering, "I have a top secret message for you of great importance." Trusting him because of his recent gift giving, the ruler sent everyone else away from his throne room. Now this ruler was a very obese man, and he went into his private summer parlor where the breezes kept his perspiration and discomfort from being overbearing to him. **Thus unguarded, the left-hander entered the parlor where only the ruler was allowed to go, and said to him, "I have a message for you."**

As the ruler stood to hear, his clever enemy removed the blade from his right thigh and plunged it deep into the stomach of his foe. Wild-eyed and in panic, the ruler frantically tried to remove the dagger, but he was so fat that the very handle sunk into him and he could not withdraw it. Thinking quickly, "Lefty" shut and locked the doors to the parlor and headed away.

After some time, the ruler's servants (who had failed to find Lefty's dagger) came to check on their lord, and finding the doors locked, they thought he must be relieving himself. They waited and waited and waited for their ruler to finish his toilet, and after so long a delay they became ashamed for him. Taking a key, they entered and found the ruler—lying dead on the ground. The left-hander used this time to carefully find his way home. Sounding the trumpet, he marshalled his people, and they slew thousands of the now leaderless enemy. Thus, a man accounted not handsome and of little worth in his own culture, wrought a great victory that brought rest to their land for eighty years.

***** *"Handsome is as handsome does."* *****

> **The Jealous Brothers**
> **("The Donkey and the Lapdog" in light of Genesis 37—47)**

A father had twelve sons, one very beloved by him. Not content, ten of the brothers became jealous of their father's special favor bestowed upon this brother, and they plotted to kill him. At the last moment, they switched their plan and sold him into slavery to a passing caravan of traders. Being taken to a mighty and influential kingdom, the despised brother proved himself faithful in many dire circumstances until he finally became second-in-command to the ruler of this vast empire.

A great famine arose around the entire world, so the father sent the ten sons to buy grain from the kingdom where his lost son was now, unknown to him, vice-regent. The father continued to mourn for his favored son, thinking him to have been slain by wild beasts (as the brothers had told their father). When the brothers arrived at the kingdom to buy grain, their now royal brother immediately recognized them, but his appearance had so changed and his authority was so great that they knew not who he was. Devising a scheme to get his father to come also, the wise and once-despised brother sent his ten brothers back home.

"You may only return if you bring your other brother," (who was the youngest and now his father's favorite). Against his own wishes, the father sent his youngest son to the faraway land. With great emotion, the brother-become-ruler revealed himself to all his brethren. He sent for his father with a great caravan filled with food and wealth, and his entire family relocated to the kingdom where he ruled. The brothers finally had the favor that they desired, and their jealousy and discontent proved to be unfounded—for the brother they sought to destroy became their very salvation.

***** *"Be content with your lot."* *****

> **The Wise Leader**
> **("The Fisherman and Troubled Water"** in light of Daniel 6**)**

A mighty emperor set up the 120 satraps in his vast kingdom under three principal leaders. Since one of the three proved to be the wisest, the emperor planned to make him ruler of all. Prompted by jealousy, the other leaders sought a way to bring their wise opponent into disrepute before the emperor, but found none. Then a wicked scheme came to them. Their enemy was a man of prayer, so they brought before their sovereign a new rule that no public prayer could be made without deference to the emperor. The emperor signed the rule into law, such a law which could not be altered or broken, and the conspirators waited for their chance.

Although knowing the potential consequences of his actions, the wise leader prayed with the windows of his home open for all to see. Scurrying with this news to the emperor, the other leaders pointed out that the punishment for breaking the rule was to be thrown into a den of hungry lions. To his horror, the emperor realized that his beloved servant must go through this deadly punishment. Thus the wise leader was sealed into the lion's den by a large stone.

After a sleepless night, the emperor ran at daybreak to the den and cried unto his servant, "Are you alive and safe?" Joyously he heard his beloved servant reply that he had been protected throughout the night. Being a just ruler, the emperor commanded that those leaders who had accused his beloved servant (along with their entire families) be cast into the lion's den—whereupon the beasts tore them to pieces and brake their bones before they even reached the bottom of the den. The very rule they had devised for hurt to their enemy became the cause of their own terrible downfall.

***** *"It was a poor rule that does not work both ways."* *****

> **The Queen's Dear Cousin**
> **("The Eagle and the Arrow" in light of Esther 1—7)**

Once, a great ruler celebrated his reign with a magnificat feast and invited all of his subjects throughout the land. Wishing to share the beauty of his queen with them, he commanded her to present herself, but she refused. Greatly angered, the ruler (at the advice of his many counselors) banned the reckless queen from his presence and sought a new bride.

Fair young girls came from the far reaches of the empire to be purified and then spend a night with the ruler. One young girl who came was cousin to one of the ruler's officers. He advised his young cousin on how to prepare to meet the ruler, and she heeded his good counsel. Endearing herself to the chief eunuch, she was taken before the ruler, who fell deeply in love with her for her beauty and good sense. Thus, she became the new queen.

At the same time, the ruler promoted another officer, and this new prestige went to the man's head. **He expected the queen's cousin to bow in homage to him, but her cousin would not dishonor his people by doing so.**

Unknown to this jealous officer, the queen's faithful cousin had some time before foiled a plot on the great ruler's life.

When the ruler asked what should be done to honor a benefactor, the officer in his selfishness assumed the ruler referred to the officer himself. He recommended a grandiose parade before the kingdom, and so the ruler told the officer to carry out his plan—in honor of the queen's cousin! Mortified, the officer did so, and then grew even more despondent at the honor shown to the queen's cousin, being filled with rage and hatred for him. **He whined about his woes to his wife and friends, and they recommended that he trap the queen's cousin and then have him hanged.**

Setting up this murderous plot by tricking the ruler, the officer went so far as to build a gallows for his hated "enemy" in public sight. When the queen learned of this vicious scheme, she invited the evil officer to a banquet, where she revealed his wicked plot before her husband the ruler. The ruler left the banquet room to think things over, and the officer frantically fell upon the queen's furniture to beg for his life.

When the ruler returned, he saw the officer ostensibly forcing the queen, and flew into a mighty rage. The ruler's men told him of the gallows prepared by the officer for the queen's cousin, and the ruler knew what he would do. He hanged this evil officer upon the very instrument of death that the officer had prepared for the queen's dear cousin.

***** *"We often give our enemies the means for our own destruction."* *****

> **The Good Young Man**
> **("The Ant and the Grasshopper" in light of Genesis 37—41)**

A good and handsome young man, as the result of many a mishap, found himself indentured in a faraway land to the captain of its king. After a short time, because of his wit and industry, the captain made this lad steward over all his house.

But the captain's wife became enraptured with the lad, and daily sought to seduce him into her bed. Despite his constant rebuffs, she persisted, and one day approached him when no other soul was in the house. She grabbed him and he fled—but she clung to his garment—and later used it as "proof" to her husband that the lad had tried to rape her. In a rage, the captain threw the lad into prison, under the care of the warden there.

Once again, the youth's good sense and honest habits brought him into the good graces of the warden, who promoted him to serve in the prison. At the same time, the king's baker and his cupbearer were thrown into prison, where both had prophetic dreams. **Unsure of their meaning both of the king's former servants sought the advice of the lad, who promptly told them the accurate meaning of their dreams—for the baker was soon hanged and the cupbearer restored to his master's care.**

Two years later, the king had two disturbing dreams—**with visions of withered plants and fetid, malnourished cattle destroying good crops and healthy livestock.**

Waking in a start, the king sought the advice of his wise men and soothsayers, but none would dare guess the meaning of the dreams. It was then that the king's cupbearer remembered the lad in prison, and he was brought before the king.

Once more giving an accurate interpretation, the lad foretold of seven years of rich harvests followed by seven years of famine. Despite the natural urge to use up all of the grain from the good years of harvest to feed the people, the ruler followed the lad's advice to save exactly twenty percent to prepare for necessity in the upcoming years of famine.

The wise youth's words came to pass, and the king not only saved his own people during worldwide want, but also fed other beleaguered nations from his store.

***** *"It is best to prepare for the days of necessity."* *****

> **The Disguised Queen**
> (**"The Vain Jackdaw"** in light of I Kings 14:1-18)

The crown prince of a large kingdom became deathly sick. His father, an evil and wicked king, came up with a plan for his recovery. **He convinced the queen to borrow different clothing and alter her appearance so that she could not be recognized.**

Then she was to visit a prophet, who although being blind was well known for divine guidance, to find out what was to become of the prince. She dutifully carried out the plan and approached the door of the prophet in her "borrowed" identity.

True to form, the prophet had received guidance that gave advanced warning of her arrival. When he heard her footsteps at his door, he asked her why she was disguised, and then proceeded to give her sad news—her beloved son, the prince, would die from his disease.

Thus the king's deceit as carried out by the queen did little to protect their family from the consequences of that ruler's evil ways.

***** *"Borrow not to fool others."* *****

➢ The True Mother
("The Wolf, the Fox and the Ape" in light of I Kings 3:16-28)

A mighty king was known not only for his great wealth, but also for his wisdom and discernment. One day, two women brought their case before him. The first woman told her story: "This woman and I live in the same home. I gave birth to a son while she was there. Three days later, she also brought forth a son in the house—and we were the only two there at that time. Well, this horrible mother rolled on top of her newborn during the night and killed it! Then to make matters worse (I can hardly bear to say it), she took her dead son and put him in my lap, and stole my living son and took him for her own. I woke the next morning to breastfeed my baby boy and found him dead. Despite my great grief, I examined the child more closely and discovered that this was not the son I bore (for a mother knows her own flesh!).

The king had listened intently, and at that point the other woman could hold her tongue no longer, but cried out, "Lies! The living child is my son, the dead child is yours!" Silencing their bitter squabbling, the king spoke with his full authority and said, "Each of you say to the other that the living son is mine and yours is dead. I will end the matter. Bring me a sword!" Immediately the king's command was carried out and he made this royal pronouncement: "Take the sword and chop the child in half. Then give a half to each of these claimants for motherhood." Hearing so harsh a sentence, the real mother of the boy yearned to save her son and cried out, "O King, spare the child and give it to this woman. I revoke my claim, that you slay the child not!" But the other woman, in her roguish and evil mood, gloated and said, "Yes! Let neither of us have the pleasure of a living son. Cut it in half before our eyes!" Thus the king saw each woman's true colors by their words and intent. **Swiftly he commanded, "Give the child to the mother who was willing to spare his life, even if it meant losing her beloved son to another. For she is the true mother of the child!"**

***** *"It is hard for a rogue to establish his innocence at any time."* *****

> **A Selfish People**
> **("The Horse and the Stag"** in light of I Kings 16:8-28**)**

A dissatisfied and indecisive people were ruled by a king for two years. At that time his servant, captain over half of the king's chariots, conspired against him. While the king was getting drunk at his steward's home, the half-captain entered and slew him—thinking to take the crown in the process. To safeguard his hopeful throne, this self-proclaimed king immediately killed every male child of his predecessor, and even wreaked vengeance on his former master's relatives and friends.

But his "reign" was a short one! Just one week later, the people heard of his foul deeds and selected a mighty captain of the kingdom's army to be their legitimate king. Accepting their charge and confidence, he rushed to the city where his foe still remained after killing his master and his master's people. Thus the newly-chosen captain and the people besieged the city so that their foe and his forces could not escape. When the half-captain saw that all of his royal dreams were to no avail, he entered his master's palace and set it aflame so that he died.

But even though the selfishness of one part of this people had cost them their lives, the remainder could not agree on who should rule them. Each faction selfishly felt that they should have the power of the throne. Half of them wanted the army captain to rule them, and the other half selected a rival.

Yet, the army captain prevailed, and ruled the people with malice and rigor. He brought the people great pain, for he did greater evil than any king that was ever before him.

***** *"Selfishness brings its own pains."* *****

> **The Four Captives**
>   **("The Lark and Her Young Ones"** in light of Daniel 1:1-21**)**

The emperor of a worldwide kingdom attacked and besieged the capital city of his enemies in a faraway land. Taking the city, the emperor raided its temple of treasures and brought back to his country many vessels made of precious metals.

Being an innovative ruler, he commanded his chief eunuch to examine members of the royal family. Those who proved to be of excellent health and noble disposition, wise in science and knowledge, and having exceptional ability were to be taken away to the empire's capital. There they were to be instructed in their captors' language and dine on the emperor's finest fare along with choice wine from the emperor's own storehouse. After three years of such rigorous education and splendid care, they were to present themselves to the emperor for his approval.

Four young men of those taken were close friends. They decided that the king's food and wine were not for them. They expressed their desire to the steward appointed by the chief eunuch to care for them, and he became alarmed, saying, "I must give you the food and wine of the emperor, for should your health suffer without it, it could cost me my life!" One of the four proposed a plan: "Let us eat our own choice of food, and drink only water, for ten days. If we are not in excellent health, we will do as you wish." This was done, and after the ten days the four young men were stronger and of greater health than any who ate and drank of the emperor's dainties. Thus, the steward gave them their own selected food and water. Helping themselves, the four grew stronger and wiser and more learned than all others. When they presented themselves to the emperor at their given time, he found them wiser and more wonderful than any taken captive before. In fact, because they relied on their own good resources, **the emperor found them "ten times better" than all the leaders or wise men in his vast empire!**

***** *"Self help is usually the best help."* *****

35

> **The Lying Escapee**
> **("The Crow and Mercury"** in light of I Samuel 31:1-6 & II Samuel 1:1-16**)**

A mighty but foolish king was sorely wounded by an arrow in the heat of battle. Fearing his enemy should fall upon him, the king begged his armorbearer to dispatch him speedily before his foes could abuse and slay him. Fearing to take such an action against his liege, his servant refused. So the king fell upon his own sword and died. Upon seeing his master's cruel fate, the armorbearer followed suit and joined him in death.

Three days later, a man fled that battle scene, and finding the king's successor, he fell at his feet. The new king saw that this man had torn clothes and dirt upon his head—a sign of great grief in those days. The escapee reported that the old king was dead. And when asked how he died, the escapee told a clever lie, hoping to gain a reward from the new king: "I chanced to come upon the king who was leaning on his spear, and the chariots of the enemy were almost upon him. He pleaded with me to slay him, since his life had not fully ebbed away in the midst of such dire circumstances. **So I killed him and took his royal crown and bracelet—and here they are!"**

Hearing so calamitous a falsehood, the new king told a young soldier nearby to fall upon and slay the man, because he had dared to kill a monarch. As the escapee died, he heard the king's bold pronouncement: "Your blood is upon your own head, for your mouth has testified of your evil."

***** *"False promises bring their own punishment."* *****

➢ **The Shameful Calf**
  ("The Silkworm and the Spider" in light of Exodus 31:1-11; 32:1-8,19-28)

Many years ago, a prophet was told to select a wise artificer to fashion tools and sacred objects that could be used for centuries. **This man was skillful with gold, silver, brass, precious stones, and could carve all manner of costly woods.**

But before the prophet could begin the project, his brother gathered the people together and that very day molded a calf of beaten gold. The people began to worship his hastily-made handiwork and claimed that it had rescued them from their enemies.

When the prophet came upon their idolatrous revelry and debauchery, he was filled with anger. Grinding the shameful idol to powder, he cast it upon the waters and forced the people to drink their former "god." Then he called for those who would stand with him, and commanded the armed guard to slay thousands of those who persisted in their evil ways. With the calf destroyed, the chosen artificer slowly and carefully crafted the sacred vessels and canopies that were then used in worship for hundreds of years, bringing blessing and prosperity to those who faithfully used them.

***** *"Time well spent is not wasted."* *****

> **The "Clever" General**
> **("The Cock and the Fox"** in light of Judges 4:1-24)

A mighty general led his 900 charioteers to overcome, for his king, a simple people and then oppressed them for twenty years. Inspired by a prophetess, a valiant hero arose from this conquered people and gathered an army of ten thousand, taking them up to a mountaintop. The general took his chariots and forces to fight his new foes along a river at the base of the mountain. But they were soon mired in the marshes along the river, so that the valiant hero led his men down the mountainside to slaughter their oppressors.

Escaping the fray, the general chanced upon the tent of a nomad, whose wife was alone there. She showed the fugitive great hospitality and allowed him to stay. He even commanded her to guard the tent entrance and tell anyone looking for the general that he was not there. Then, taking advantage of her kindness, and for fear of being discovered, the general cunningly hid himself in the woman's portion of the tent—which was to that people, a violation of custom worthy of death.

When he had fallen asleep, she discovered his vulgar breach of honor, and carried out the required judgment. **Taking a hammer and tent stake, she quietly crept up to her guest and drove the stake into his head.**

When the valiant leader arrived looking for the general, the nomad's wife showed him his foe, fastened to the earth like the tent in which he lay. Thus, the general's "clever" plan led to his own demise.

***** *"Cunning often outwits itself."* *****

> **The Lustful Prince and His False Friend**
> **("The Sick Stag" in light of II Samuel 13:1-39)**

A king had many wives, **and one of the princes fell in love with his stepsister, greatly desiring to have her.**

This prince had a "best friend" who was very cunning. When the friend noticed that the prince was losing weight and constantly sad, he asked of his welfare. The prince told him of his infatuation with the princess, and the friend came up with a plan. Carrying out the prescribed deception in every detail, the prince pretended to be ill and waited for the king to visit him.

When his father came to his bedside, the prince requested that this stepsister come to his room, make some bread there, and feed it to him. The king, seeing no apparent evil in such a request, asked his daughter to do so—and she willingly complied. But after she had kindly prepared and baked the food, the prince refused to eat it. He sent all the men away from his outer room and asked his stepsister to come into the privacy of his bedroom to feed him.

There, he grabbed her and said, "Come and lie with me!" The princess was horrified at the thought of having such relations forced upon her and cried out, "No! Please do not force yourself upon me, for this ought not to be done in our land. How would I bear such shame, and would you not be considered to be a fool by all who hear of this? If you ask the king's permission, could we not then marry and share love?"

But the prince was filled with carnal desire and, being stronger than his stepsister, viciously raped her in his own bed.

Once his lust had been satisfied, his whole attitude changed—he now hated the princess even more than he had previously wanted her. With callous heart, he ordered her from his room. But the ruined girl sadly begged him, "There is no reason for me to leave now that you have had me. This evil in sending me away is greater than the deed you have already done." The prince hardened his heart and refused her entreaties, then ordered one of his servants to throw his stepsister out and lock the door behind her.

When another prince, the girl's blood brother, heard of this foul deed, he plotted carefully to avenge his sister's honor. After two full years, he found an opportunity and slew the lustful prince for what he had done to his sister. False rumors flew around the palace that all of the king's sons had been slain, and the king was distraught.

But the supposed "caring and true friend" who had devised the scheme and rape, told the king that only the lustful prince was slain, and that was because of what he had done to the princess. **Thus, this so-called friend not only cost a prince his life, but tried to use such a relation to gain the king's ear for his own selfish advantage.**

***** *"It is easy to judge your true friends by the amount of care they exercise for your welfare."* *****

> **A Turn of Events**
> (**"The Eagle and the Beetle"** in light of Exodus 1:1-22)

A wise and noble foreigner journeyed to a kingdom and there advised the king on how to survive a bitter famine. In thankfulness for his service, the king gave him great wealth and position—and even brought in his large family, giving them the finest of the land to dwell in. The foreigner and his many relatives prospered and became mighty in the land.

Later, a new king, who had not known the foreigner nor seen the salvation that he brought to the kingdom, became alarmed at the power this man's race had gained. Meeting with his counselors, the king decided to enslave these people, putting them under the lash to build his new cities. But even in their servitude, these "foreigners" continued to multiply, much to the dismay of the king.

So the king, taking another tack, called in the midwives who birthed the alien people that he so hated. He commanded them to kill every boy that was born, and to allow the girls to live. Thus, he planned to use infanticide to keep this people enslaved by having no male heirs to carry on th eir line.

But the midwives, taking courage against so evil an order, allowed the male children to live. When the king confronted them, they simply replied, **"These women are not as your race, for they are so strong that they have already had their children before we arrive!"**

Finding no fault with the midwives, the king let them go to live fruitful lives. And this "weak" people that he so hated, continued to prosper, so that one day they arose against the king and powerfully conquered him and his entire army.

***** *"The weak often revenge themselves on those who use them ill, even though they be more powerful."* *****

> **The Ungrateful Landowner**
> **("The Ass, the Dog and the Wolf"** in light of I Samuel 25:1-42)

A band of kind outlaws used their forces to protect the herdsmen of a local landowner. When this wealthy farmer went to shear his sheep, the leader of the outlaws sent men to ask a small share from the land's bounty—which their master could have easily given. But the landowner refused to share of his plenty, and even gravely insulted the outlaw leader's reputation before the messengers.

Reporting his words to their master, their leader commanded his forces to strap on their weapons and to wreak vengeance upon so vile an ingrate. But a wise young servant of the landowner told his master's wife about the evil her husband had done.

Realizing the consequences that would follow, the wife took food and drink and met the outlaw leader as he approached her home. She pleaded with him for the lives of her family and household, and spoke many encouraging words that melted his heart and softened his wrath.

Thanking her, the leader departed, after the landowner's wife had asked him to remember her deed. She returned to find her husband drunken and feasting, so she waited until morning light to give him the news. When he learned of the foiled attack and his near brush with death, **his heart sank within him like a stone, and he died ten days later.**

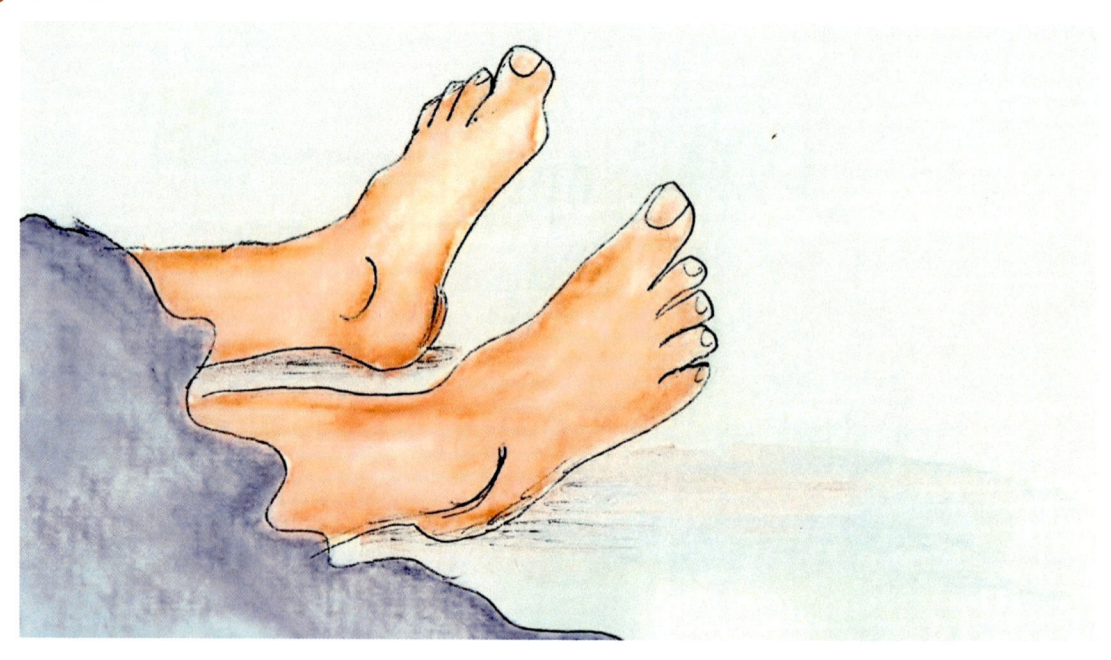

Hearing of the landowner's death, the outlaw leader took this evil man's widow to wife and loved her dearly. She received his kind attentions for her help to him, gaining enduring rewards from the man that her wicked husband had so foolishly cast aside.

***** *"Not to help others has no rewards."* *****

➤ The Unfaithful Guests
("The Thrush and the Swallow" in light of I Kings 1:1-49)

A famous king had grown old and was near death. One of his elder sons conspired to take the throne and gathered together an army captain, a political leader, and a priest to help him. With these influential men on his side, he called the king's sons and the people of the land to a grand feast—but he slighted his younger brother and did not invite him or his supporters.

A wise prophet told the mother of the younger prince of her son's plight, and advised her to approach the king and ask him to give her son the crown. With the help of the prophet, she spoke with the king, and he called for a grand coronation for her son. Many people from the kingdom attended the affair, and as he was crowned they cheered so loudly that the earth shook.

When those who were feasting with their "friend," the elder prince, heard the shouting, they wondered what it meant. **When they learned of the coronation, and realized that they had backed the wrong son, they became greatly afraid, and each rose up to skulk away to his own home.**

Being deserted by all his fair-weather guests, the elder prince became afraid and ran for his life.

***** *"Do not take fair weather friendships seriously."* *****

> **The Blind Man and the Prophet**
> **("The Wind and the Sun"** in light of John 9:1-41**)**

A mighty prophet found a man who was blind from birth, and by divine power healed him. When the local religious leaders saw that the man had regained his sight, they asked him how it had occurred. When he told them of the prophet, they doubted the man's words—for they did not consider the prophet to be "good enough" to perform such deeds.

Dragging his parents before them, the religious leaders asked them if this was their son who was born blind, and how he could now see. Of course, they knew what the prophet had done, but for fear of public ridicule and of being ostracized from their religious community, they said it was indeed their son—but that they did not know how he could now see. Still not satisfied, the religionists brought the man himself before them again to severely interrogate him. **Growing tired of their constant rants, he boldly affirmed who had healed him.**

With that, they cast the formerly blind man from their presence, laying their condemnation upon him. A short time later, the prophet (who was also the promised deliverer for all mankind) found the man he had healed, and in a kindly manner gave him even greater insight and salvation—far beyond the physical sight he had initially gained.

***** *"Kindness affects more than severity."* *****

➢ **The Corrupted Seer**
   ("The Spaniel and the Mastiff" in light of Numbers 22—24 & Joshua 13:22)

An ancient Seer gained a reputation for his connection with the divine. Hoping to prosper by the Seer's aid, a king asked him to curse his enemies. But the Seer's guidance was that he should not help the king.

Next, the wicked king offered to promote the Seer to great honor and wealth. This time, the Seer's guidance was to go with the king's men if they should approach him. **Being zealous for the promised reward, the Seer sought out the king's men first and journeyed with them to befriend the king.**

On the way, he refused to listen any longer to the guidance given him, even when his donkey spoke to him and urged him to turn back.

The Seer spoke forth four separate oracles for the king, and to his royal friend's consternation, they blessed rather than cursed the king's enemy. Having been spellbound by the king's bribes, the Seer had established a friendship with the king. Sometime later, having chosen to associate with such a perverse and evil king, the Seer died at the hands of the very people he had been paid to curse.

***** *"Choose your friends well."* *****

> **Lesson from a Gourd**
> (**"The Dog in the Manger"** in light of Jonah 1—4)

After a phenomenal journey, a traveling prophet came unto the capital city of a giant empire. This empire was much more powerful than the prophet's home country, and proved a threat to it. He was commanded to speak to the people living in the empire's capital so that they would change their evil ways. Contrary to what the prophet wished, the people did repent and were saved from destruction. Thus, the nation was free to continue their conquests, which could someday include the prophet's own people.

Thinking that his people might someday suffer for their lack of repentance, the prophet sat dejectedly under the shadow of a vine which produced a gourd. Taking shelter from the hot sun in the gourd's shadow, the prophet felt better. But soon a worm struck the gourd so that it died, and the prophet once more felt the sun's mighty rays. The heat was so intense that, coupled with a strong east wind, the prophet wished to die.

Then he realized how foolish he was. He felt great remorse for a gourd that he did not even plant, and had no pity for the penitent thousands in the city who had been spared. He had begrudged the empire the peace they meekly deserved, which he knew his own people (in their lack of humility) would later refuse and never enjoy.

***** *"People often grudge others what they cannot enjoy themselves."* *****

➢ **The Four Young Rebels**
   (**"The Thirsty Pigeon"** in light of Numbers 16:1-50)

Four young tribal leaders were zealous to command the people, and grew tired of submitting to the leadership of their elders. Bringing 250 well-known men with them, **they withstood the two most prominent elders to the face—elders who had oftentimes proven themselves with supernaturally powerful deeds.**

It was decided that the next day, the men from each opposing party would stand apart from each other in order to see, by some work of power, which group was worthy to be followed.

When the elders called the four rebels out the next day, two refused to even come to the contest. So the elders told the people to step away from the tents of the upstarts. Many people moved away, and the rebel youths and their families stood before their tents.

Suddenly, a mighty earthquake rent the ground about their tents, and the youths (along with their families and all they owned) were swallowed up, never to be seen again. And the 250 renowned men who had joined them were struck by lightning and burned to a crisp. Thus their zeal to lead outran the discretion that they needed with men of such power.

***** *"Zeal should not outrun discretion."* *****

> **The Courageous Innkeeper**
> **("The Fox and the Countryman"** in light of Joshua 2:1-14; 6:1-27)

The victorious general of an invading army sent two spies into a city he hoped to soon besiege and conquer. Finding an inn along the city wall, they sought refuge there. But the city's king had spies of his own who learned of the men's presence in his city. This king sent messengers to order the innkeeper to give up the two spies, but she secretly hid them in some crops drying upon her roof.

She told the king's messengers, "I did see the men that you seek, but they left near nightfall when the city gates are closed. I don't know where they went, but if you hurry, you may still catch them!" So the king's men set out in hopeful pursuit to the banks of a river, and the city gate was shut tightly behind them.

Before they could lie down for the evening, the innkeeper met the spies upon the roof and told them how she and many in the city had heard of the general's many military victories. She promised to help them escape the city, if they in turn would save her and her family when the city was later taken by the general. **The two spies agreed to her terms, so she let them down by a rope outside her inn upon the wall, and she also told them where and how long to hide from the pursuers.**

They followed her plan and safely returned to the general. When the general and his forces did besiege and overrun the city, the spies found the innkeeper and rescued her and her family, as they had promised. Although her words to the king's messengers were of no value to them, her brave actions helped to bring the general great victory and saved her family from destruction.

***** *"Actions speak louder than words."* *****

> **A Narrow Escape**
> **("The Spendthrift and the Swallow"** in light of I Samuel 19:1-18)

An evil king became jealous of his general and sought to kill him. Even though the general was married to the king's daughter, he persisted in his attempts. One day, the king in his rage threw a javelin at the general, hoping to smite him to the wall. Although he missed, the king felt sure that he could easily kill him the next time that he tried.

That night, he surrounded the couple's home with his soldiers. But the king's daughter warned her husband (for she loved him dearly) and secretly let him down through a window so that he escaped.

The next day, the soldiers entered and saw the general's form in his bed, for his wife had used pillows and an image covered with a blanket to fool them. She told the soldiers that her husband was sick, and they reported back to the king. Losing his patience, the king commanded that the general be brought to him, bed and all, so that he might slay him. **But when the soldiers returned, they found the pillows and image—and no general!**

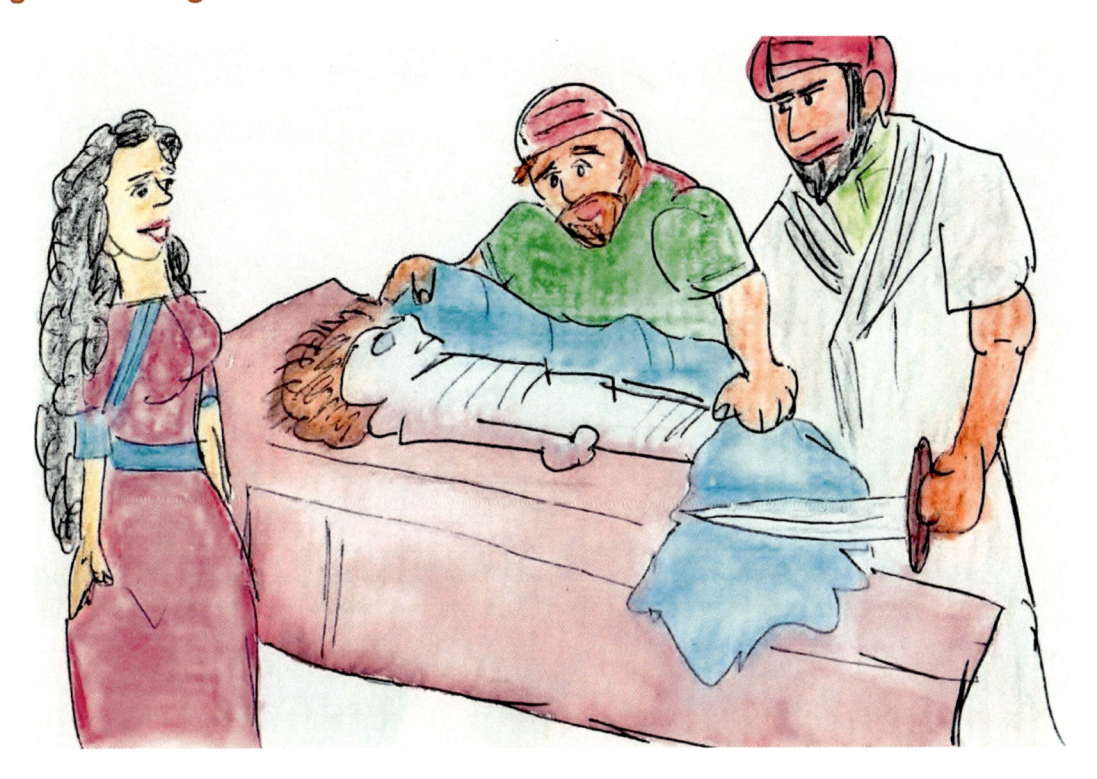

The king railed on his daughter and asked her why she had deceived her father and helped his enemy. To save herself from her father's wrath, she claimed that her husband threatened her life if she would not help him escape. Thus, the king's overconfidence allowed his hated enemy to go free.

***** *"One swallow does not make a summer."* *****

➤ **The Slain Giant**
  ("The Hunter, the Fox, and the Tiger" in light of I Samuel 17:1-58)

A giant towered over every other person in his country, as well as in the nations that surrounded it. He became a powerful warrior and could easily kill anyone who dared to face him. One day, his army squared off against their foes, with troops arrayed on either side of a small valley.

Using his usual bravado, the giant challenged the rival army in hectoring tones so that they quaked in fear at his reprisals. But then, a small and ruddy youth stepped up, armed with only a sling. **The giant, thinking the youth to be an easy match, laughed him to scorn and cursed him by his gods.**

But the boy showed no fear. When the giant threatened to feed the youth to the birds of the air and the beasts of the field, the young shepherd answered in kind, telling the giant that he would soon have his head.

The giant lumbered forward and the youth ran boldly toward him, slinging a stone taken from the riverbed. With amazing accuracy, the stone slammed into the greaves of the giant's leg armor, causing him to topple forward. Weighted down by his heavy armor, the giant lay helpless as the youth took the giant's own sword and, with one swift blow, beheaded his proud opponent. Seeing their champion overcome, the giant's army fled in terror and was soundly beaten in its retreat.

***** *"Do not always take things for granted."* *****

➢ **The Flattering Prince**
   ("The Hen and the Fox" in light of II Samuel 15:1-18; 18:15-17)

An ancient king had many sons. **One of the princes stood daily outside the royal judgment chamber and spoke to those who came to petition the king.**

The prince would question them about where they were from and the reason they came to see his father. Flattering them with promised help, the prince built a network of allegiance and dependency upon himself among many of the kingdom's subjects.

After doing this for forty years, the prince's flattering words had garnered so much support that he openly rebelled from his father, the king, who had to flee for his life. Later the prince was defeated, and his followers were disbanded.

Thus his flattering words brought them temporary opportunity, but cost them their safety in the long run.

***** *"Those who will not listen to flatterers will have a safer life."* *****

> **The Resentful Captain**
> **("The Angler and the Little Fish" in light of II Kings 5:1-14)**

There once was a valorous captain over his king's army who won many victories—but suffered from a supposedly incurable disease. It so happened that his wife had a handmaid who had been captured from a foreign land. "If only your husband, my lord, could see the holy man from my homeland, he would be healed of his disease," she said to the captain's wife. When the captain heard of this hope for his recovery, he asked his king for help. The captain's king sent word to the ruler of the maid's homeland, requesting that he send someone to heal the captain. At first, the ruler thought the king was attempting to provoke a war by asking for "impossible" help in curing the captain. But the holy man, known to the handmaid, told the dubious ruler to send the captain to him. When the captain arrived, he was met by the holy man's servant who told him to simply wash in the local stream—and he would be healed of his disease. But the captain flew into a rage, "What!" he cried, "Will this holy man not come out himself and make a magnificent show of power and heal my disease before all? Why should I wash in this dirty little stream, when our nation has clear rushing mountain rivers? **Can I not wash at home and be clean?**"

So he stalked off in a huff. Then his servants approached him with some calm and sound advice. "O beloved lord, if the holy man had asked you to perform some magnificent feat, would you have not gladly complied? He simply asks you to wash in this stream that is close at hand. Is that not simpler and better than waiting for some prospective display in the future?" The captain saw the wisdom in their words and put off his dreams of a grandiose ceremony. He washed in the local stream as the holy man had said, and he was completely healed of his disease. In fact, his body was healthier than ever before!

***** *"A little thing in hand is worth more than a great thing in prospect."* *****

> **The Foolhardy Twin**
> **("The Fox and the Grapes"** in light of Genesis 25:19-34)

A pregnant woman noticed a "struggling" within her womb and sought divine guidance as to what it should mean. She learned that each child within her would someday become a great leader, but that the first to come out would serve the second.

When the twins were born, the first boy was hairy and the second was grasping his brother by the heel. As the boys grew, the mother noticed that indeed the second was intuitive and God-fearing, while his older brother trusted in his mighty prowess and hunting skills. The father loved the "firstborn" (although he was actually born shortly before his "younger" brother) and the wild game he would bring his father to eat. But though he was firstborn, he had little use for taking on family leadership and did not see himself as a spiritual leader.

Thus one day, when the older brother returned from the field in great hunger, he desired to have the delicious soup that his brother had prepared that day. The younger said he could have some, but he must surrender his birthright claim as leader. The elder replied, "I am starving, so what good is a leadership title to me?" The younger persisted with his demand, "Swear to me that you will hand over to me this birthright claim!" The elder swore he would and hungrily devoured the food. Thus he despised as little worth what he felt was not within his grasp to achieve.

***** *"It is easy to despise what you cannot get."* *****

> **The Dishonest Father-in-law**
> **("The Man and the Lion" in light of Genesis 31:1-55)**

A young man fell in love with a local shepherd girl and asked for her hand in marriage. Her father agreed, but on the wedding night, he secretly put his older daughter in her place. The next day, the unsuspecting groom was surprised at his new wife, and complained of the father's trickery. So the father agreed to give him both daughters if he worked for seven years for each of them. After serving for twenty years, and after both sisters and their handmaids had many children, the young man tried to escape his father-in-law's deceitful ways by stealing away at night.

Three days later, his father-in-law learned of his escape and followed him for a full week before catching the young man. The elder painted the situation from his point of view: "Why have you run away and taken my daughters and their children and the flocks I gave you? Do you not know that I have the power to hurt you?"

But the young man spoke truly in response: "For twenty years I have guarded your flocks and replaced any beast that was harmed or killed. I have served you fourteen years for your daughters and six more years for your cattle. You have changed my wages ten times! And you had planned to send me away with nothing."

***** *"We can easily represent things as we wish them to be."* *****

➢ The Unthankful People
("The Sheep and the Dog" in light of Numbers 11:1-35)

A prophet rescued thousands of slaves who had been in bondage under a wicked king. During their journey to a new home, they were regularly fed, but complained about their food. The prophet saw that a grain was miraculously provided to make bread each day.

Even though they were well off, this too was not good enough for the people. They complained that they needed "real meat," and thus it came to them—**quails were blown by a strong wind to their camp so they could catch them by the thousands!**

And so they ate this way for a month, until a great plague fell upon them, and many died because of their lusting and unthankful hearts.

***** *"When one is well off it is not proper to complain."* *****

> **The Unfaithful Relatives**
> **("The Wolf in Disguise"** in light of Judges 12:1-7)

A mighty warrior defeated his enemy after passing through his family's land. Later, some of the relatives complained that they had not been invited to join him in the battle, and threatened to burn his house down with him in it.

Such evil language and wicked character! He told them that they had failed to help him when he asked, so that he alone had to take on their common enemy. Thus unable to agree, the warrior and his family waged war on each other.

The warrior's men guarded the mountain passes and when the relatives tried to go through, they asked them to pronounce a certain word. Because their dialect was different, they said that word with an unusual accent and revealed who they were.

Thus the warrior slew his unfaithful relatives—who had indeed betrayed themselves not only by their bad character, but also by the way they spoke.

***** *"Character is often determined by your language."* *****

➢ **The Besieged City**
   ("The Hares and the Frogs" in light of II Kings 7:1-16)

A great royal city was under siege by a mighty army so that the inhabitants were near death from starvation. Four men sat at the gate of the city and said to each other: "Why do we sit here until we die? If we enter into the city we will die from famine, and if we stay here we will also be killed. Let's go to the enemy camp and surrender ourselves. If they kill us, we are no worse off than our other choices—for we will only die. That is better than starving within the city."

So at twilight they snuck in to the enemy camp and found the outer tents abandoned (for the enemy army had fled in terror having heard a false report of impending defeat). The four men were so famished that they ate and drank of the food they found there. Seeing great wealth in the tents around them, they grabbed silver and gold and rich clothing and hid it, hoping to recover it later.

But then their consciences began to bother them, as they realized those in the city were in much worse straights than they were. **"This should be a day of rejoicing. If we continue here until morning perhaps some evil will befall us. We will tell the king!"**

So they approached the gatekeeper of the city and they were brought to the king. Hearing their report, the king sent out scouts to check their story, and it was all true. So the siege was lifted and the people ate heartily, thankful for the riches and booty they took from the enemy camp.

***** "There is always someone worse off than yourself." *****

> **The Complaining Travelers**
> **("The Countryman and the Snake"** in light of Exodus 15:22—17:7)

Traveling through the desert, a large company complained to their leader about the lack of water. Coming upon a spring, they found the water bitter. So the people complained again. Their resourceful leader found a way to purify the water and the people quenched their thirst.

But soon they began to complain about their hunger, saying it would have been better to be slaves and be well fed than free and starving. Once again, their leader came to their aid and found food for them each day.

Yet this wicked and ungrateful people, beginning to thirst, berated their leader, asking why he had brought them and their families to the desert to die of thirst.

And once again he helped them, despite their foolish complaints.

***** *"No gratitude from the wicked."* *****

➢ The Noble Exile
("The Wolf and the Kid" in light of II Samuel 15:1—16:14)

A king was deposed by his son and forced to leave the capital city where he had reigned. On his way out of the city with his retinue of soldiers and supporters, the king was met by a former enemy.

This man cursed the king from afar, called him horrible names, and threw stones at the king and his men (all from a safe distance).

One of the king's soldiers asked the king permission to go and kill such a spiteful foe. But the king refused, saying, "I will expect future justice from this man's cursing someday." Thus the exiled king bravely ignored his enemy's foolish ravings and found shelter for himself and his people.

***** *"It is easy to be brave from a safe distance."* *****

> **The Treacherous King and His Family**
> **("The Fox and the Wolf"** in light of Judges 9:1-57**)**

A mighty leader defeated his foes and then reigned over his people. Upon his death, the eldest son went to his maternal grandfather and asked him for help. "Ask the people of your city if they want all seventy of my father's sons to rule over them, or just me—for I am their own flesh and blood on my mother's side."

The people hearkened unto the eldest son's offer, and gave him seventy pieces of silver. Using the money, he treacherously hired worthless and vain assassins who slew his brothers (although the youngest escaped). The men of the city made the eldest son their king, and he ruled over them for three years.

But then, the men of the city dealt treacherously with their new king and set up robbers in the mountains to harass the king's people. So the king besieged their city, beat down its walls, and then burned up these people where they were hiding within the hold of the city. Howbeit, as he was finishing his campaign, the king besieged another city and approached the tower where the inhabitants had fled.

Hoping to burn the tower down, the king drew close to the door, and a woman dropped a millstone upon his head from above. Mortally wounded with a crushed skull, the king begged his young armorbearer to finish him off. So the young man thrust him through, ending his treacherous reign.

***** *"Security is not gotten by treachery."* *****

➢ The Disobedient Ruler
("The Fox and the Lion" in light of I Samuel 8—15)

A coalition of tribes requested that their religious leader anoint a king from among them. When the time came for the coronation, the chosen man was hiding—thinking himself to be unworthy of so great an honor. Humbly accepting the kingship, he returned to his home with a group of supporters, and did not even confront those who spoke evil of him. **After a military victory, the new king had a triumphant coronation to reestablish his kingdom.**

Two years later, the king was fighting a neighboring kingdom, and sought the help of the religious leader. The king was told to wait for the leader to come and offer a special sacrifice. But growing anxious, and thinking he could do better, the king offered the sacrifice himself. Arriving on the scene, the religious leader saw the king's prideful action, but gave him another chance to rule.

The king gathered a large army, and the religious leader told him to totally wipe out an evil nation dwelling near their land. Again contemptuously thinking he knew better, the king saved some of the spoil and even allowed the enemy king to live. When the religious leader found this out, he slew the enemy king, and reproved his prideful protégée. Eventually, the king (who was once humble and respectful to the religious leader) was removed from his kingship for his familiarity and disobedience.

***** *"Familiarity breeds contempt."* *****

> **The Wise Judge**
> **("The Thief and the Dog" in light of Exodus 18:1-27)**

A holy man, both prophet and judge, would hear the cases of his people for hours on end, from the smallest matter to the greatest. For he wanted each case to be handled honestly and justly, and there were thousands of people in the land.

His father-in-law visited him and noticed the judge's exhaustion after a full day of audiences with the people. "What are you doing, my son?" he said. **"You will wear away if you persist in this manner. You cannot do this alone."**

He continued, "Here is my advice. Find honest and true men who cannot be bribed. Set them over the people to judge the smaller matters, and when they have a difficult case they can bring it to you. That way, you will not be worn out with daily and constant requests."

The judge searched diligently, and with divine guidance, found men who naturally loved to serve others and who refused to be bribed. They took care of the smaller cases honestly, and brought those they could not handle to the judge. Thus, justice was served and the judge did an even better job than before.

***** *"It's impossible to bribe a natural servant."* *****

➤ The Cowardly Spies
("The Frogs Desiring a King" in light of Numbers 13—14)

The leader of a nation numbering in the millions was tasked with finding them a new home. He sent twelve spies (one per tribe) into the neighboring lands to see what course they should take. Upon their return, all twelve described great riches and abundance in the surrounding countries. **However, ten of the spies quaked in fear at the inhabitants they had observed when reconnoitering.**

In contrast, two of the spies courageously claimed such an enemy could be conquered. Forsaking this brave report, the people believed the cowardly spies and spoke of deposing the leader and finding a new captain. They even cruelly desired to rule the situation and return to a land of slavery where they had once lived.

But the leader took charge and proclaimed that those spies and people who were too afraid to take the land would die before they reached it. And the two faithful spies and the young people yet to be born would one day enjoy the riches of the land. Led by divine guidance, the leader warned the people not to attack these neighboring lands. But they did not listen, wishing to rule themselves, and were sorely beaten in battle.

***** *"Better no rule than cruel rule."* *****

➢ The Proud and Foolish Ruler
("The Ass and the Lion Hunting" in light of Daniel 5:1-31)

The proud ruler of a vast and mighty empire was known for his lavish feasts and foolhardy claims. Inviting a thousand guests, he brought them vessels of gold and silver filled with wine, and foolishly pretended that these precious metals were gods themselves. But as he proudly looked about in his drunken stupor, there appeared to the ruler, the fingers of a man's hand writing on the wall!

He sobered immediately and his knees knocked together in fright. **Summoning his wise men, he commanded them to interpret the writing that was still clearly seen upon the wall.**

Despite his promise of wealth and acclaim, none could do so. Until finally a wise man, who had served the ruler's father, rejected the proffered rewards and boldly told the ruler what the writing meant: "Your kingdom will end, for you are found wanting; it will be divided and given to others." That very night the foolish ruler was slain, and his kingdom was taken by another.

***** *"Do not be proud of being a fool."* *****

> **The Murderous Ruler and the Astronomers**
> **("The Fowler and the Birds" in light of Matthew 2:1-16)**

An ancient prophecy promised the birth of a savior for all mankind. A guild of sacred astronomers had been instructed for centuries about the signs that would appear in the sky near the time of this long-awaited birth. Finally, the astronomers saw the anticipated celestial display and journeyed across mountains and deserts to the kingdom spoken of in the prophecy.

Upon their arrival, the ruling king (an evil and vicious tyrant) accepted an audience with the astronomers to learn more of this "king" that threatened his personal rule. Learning that the child had been born in a small town near the capital city more than a year before, **he sent the astronomers there to find the child.**

With feigned emotion, he asked them to return and tell him where to find the child so that he could worship him (in reality, he planned to slay the young child and rid himself of his supposed usurper). The king's show of pity was only a cover for his wicked and murderous heart.

On the other hand, the astronomers found the child, but were warned by divine guidance not to return to the king. Seeing that his plan for finding the child's exact whereabouts had been foiled, he sent his soldiers to the town, and they killed every male child who was under two years of age. However, the prophesied savior had been safely taken away by his parents, for they too were divinely warned to escape.

***** *"True pity is not to be judged by tears."* *****

> **Worthless Wealth**
> **("The Covetous Man"** in light of Acts 12:20-23)

A wealthy king assembled his subjects to make an oration. The king wore his royal robes and proudly displayed his finery. He sat upon a great throne to show all the riches that he had.

The people shouted and proclaimed their king's greatness and the magnificence of his wealth and kingdom. "He speaks as if he were a god, and not merely human," they said.

But even as his subjects praised him, his body was infested with a loathsome disease so that this "magnificent" king was eaten of worms. He soon died, and all the wealth he was so proud of, did him little good.

***** *"Wealth unused might as well not exist."* *****

> **The King and His Captive**
> **("The Fox and the Cock" in light of Exodus 17:8-16 & I Samuel 15:1-33)**

A roving nation wished to pass through a territory, but the inhabitants of that land attacked them. After a hard-fought battle, the rovers proved triumphant and later found a place to establish their country. When they had been there a long time, they made a king for themselves. A prophet told the king that now was the time to totally wipe out their enemies for their former maliciousness.

But the king rejected the mandate, for although he killed many of the people, he helped the captured enemy ruler to live. When the prophet found this out, he came to the king and reproved him for his foolishness. Then the prophet had the captured ruler brought before him.

This wicked captive assumed that the prophet would be as "soft" as the king had been, and approached him delicately. Taking a sword in hand, the prophet cried out, "As your sword has made our people childless, so shall your mother be childless among women!" And he chopped to pieces the captured ruler in the sight of all.

***** *"No help should be given to the wicked."* *****

➢ **The Presumptuous Servant**
   ("The Dog Invited to Supper" in light of Esther 3:1; 7:1-10)

A noble emperor promoted a servant (who was clever with his words) and made him to sit above all the princes. Although he was given great authority, he was a base and foul scoundrel at heart.

Being invited to dine with the emperor and his queen, the servant's previous evil deeds toward the queen's family were exposed.

The emperor left the banquet room and entered the royal garden to consider his servant's fate.

Pleading with many words for his life, the servant (contrary to all protocol and decency) followed the queen into her chamber, even going into her bed. When the emperor returned, he was shocked at the servant's audaciously presumptive manner and cried out, "Will you forcibly assault my wife the queen in my very presence? Here in my own house?" The king's guard immediately covered the servant's head, and he was soon hanged to the death.

***** *"Manners always speak louder than words."* *****

> **The Disrespectful Youths**
> **("The Bear and the Fowls"** in light of II Kings 2:15-25**)**

A spiritual leader inherited understanding from his master so that he showed forth great power. On one occasion, when the people had founded a new city in a pleasant location, they found that the water source there was polluted. So the spiritual leader took salt and, casting it in the spring, "healed" the waters so that they were potable.

Afterward, the leader came to another city where several rowdy and disrespectful young men began to berate and mock him. "Get out of here, you empty-headed fool!" they cried. Noticing their irreverent outbursts, the leader took away his blessing from them.

Suddenly, two she-bears emerged from the forest and chased forty-two of the young men away. The spiritual leader continued on his route and helped the inhabitants of other cities along the way.

***** *"Only the ill-bred mock at others."* *****

> ### The Dissatisfied Ruler
> ### ("The Peacock and Juno" in light of I Kings 21:1-29)

A king who owned immense gardens noticed a beautiful vineyard near his palace and wanted to turn it into an herb garden. Approaching his neighbor, he offered him money or another plot of land in exchange for the property. But the neighbor refused, saying, "This is my family inheritance. It would be shameful to sell it to another."

So the discontented king returned home, pouting and whimpering that he could not have the best of everything. Then he went to his bed, turned away from everyone, and refused to eat. The queen asked him why he was in such a snit, and he told her about his failed real estate plans. Then she cried out (for she was a wicked and desperately evil witch), **"Are you not the king? I will get this land for you!"**

Using the king's own seal, she sent letters to the elders of the neighbor's city, and commanded them to have a special feast—and to make sure the king's neighbor was set up front in public view. The elders agreed, and the evil queen hired vain and cruel men to speak falsely about the king's neighbor. On the day of the special feast, these liars accused the king's neighbor of blasphemy, and the neighbor was murdered for his supposed "crime."

Inwardly rejoicing at this vile deed, the queen proudly told her husband that he could now buy the vineyard of his dreams, for its former owner was dead. But a curse came upon the king, and his descendants were later killed, as was the evil witch.

***** **"Be content with your lot; one cannot be first in everything."** *****

➢ **The False "Prophet"**
   ("The Fox in the Well" **in light of I Kings 13:1-34**)

A godly man boldly approached an evil king and spoke a divine pronouncement against him. After a mighty show of healing, the man turned to leave, and the king offered him a reward. But he replied, "I will not stay for a bite of food or a sip of drink. For I have been divinely instructed not to eat or drink with anyone, and to not even take the same route home that I used to get here."

So he headed back another way, according to the guidance he had been given. When a false and foolish old "prophet" (whose life was difficult and obscure) heard of this man's deeds with the king, he sought out and found the godly man upon his journey. He asked the traveler to dine and stay at his home, but the godly man refused—telling the "prophet" that he was forbidden to do so.

This deceitful "prophet" told the traveler that he too received divine guidance, and that an angel had straightly told him to invite the traveler to his home. Falling prey to the lie, the traveler followed the advice and ate and slept at the old man's home. In the morning, he saddled his donkey and began his journey afresh, **but he was attacked by a lion and killed.**

Hearing of this, the false prophet buried the traveler, hoping that he might gain some magical advantage from his corpse. But things only grew worse in the land.

***** *"Never trust the advice of a man in difficulties."* *****

> **The Foolish Twin**
> **("The Mocking Bird" in light of Genesis 27:1—28:9)**

A couple had twin sons who were very different in character. The firstborn was wild and loved the outdoors. His brother was thoughtful and an able leader. Their mother had been given divine insight even before the twins were born that the younger would one day rule over the elder son. She helped the second-born secure his father's blessing, which sent the older brother into a rage.

Fearing for the younger son's life, she convinced her husband to send him away to find a suitable wife from among her near relatives in another land. They did so, but the couple was constantly harangued by the lack of character in their oldest son—for he married local women who had no spiritual understanding.

When the elder brother saw that his parents were disappointed in his choice of brides, and that his younger brother had been given a blessing and sent to his mother's relatives to find a wife, he sought another wife from his father's distant relatives (hoping to imitate his brother's good deeds). But she too was without true understanding.

***** *"To only imitate does not create great character."* *****

➢ **The Talking Donkey**
  ("The Ass Laden with Salt and with Sponges" in light of Numbers 22:1-33)

A king became alarmed when a mighty nation (which had easily defeated another local kingdom) pitched their camp near him. He sent for a Seer to come and curse his enemies, but the Seer was divinely told not to do so.

The king redoubled his efforts and sent messengers with bribes to entice the Seer, who agreed to come to the king, hoping for gain. The Seer supposed this to be an "easy way" to wealth.

But as he journeyed upon his donkey, an angel brandishing a sword withstood them in the road. The Seer did not even see the angel—but the donkey did! Running away from the road, the donkey hurried into a local vineyard and found an escape route between two walls. But soon the route narrowed so that the donkey got stuck between the walls, and the Seer's foot was crushed amidst the donkey's frantic maneuvers.

Taking his staff in hand, the Seer began to beat the donkey, which began to speak as a person! **She upbraided the Seer, crying, "Why have you beaten me?"**

Then the Seer saw the angel and fell to the ground in terror. "You fool," thundered the angel, "I have withstood you on this misguided journey. Had not your donkey seen me and escaped, you would now be dead, and only she would be alive!"

***** *"The easy way is not always the best."* *****

➢ **The Widow's Story**
   ("The Stag in the Ox Stall" in light of II Samuel 14:1-20)

A prince killed his step brother, who had physically abused the prince's sister. Being banished by the king for this murder, the prince convinced the king's chief general to intercede for him. Devising a subtle plan, the general had a woman disguise herself as a widow and sent her to petition the king.

Once there, she told the king the story that the general had given her. "My Lord," she said, "I am a widow. I had two sons who argued while out in the field, and one killed his brother. My whole family is calling for the life of my only son that is left. But he is all I have left in this world." "Don't worry," promised the king, "I will see that you and your son are safe." But the woman persisted with the general's words: "How can I be cared for and yet the royal family be guilty in such a matter? Should not the king take home his banished son?" **But the king perceived who had prompted her to speak so.**

"Is not my general's hand in this, has he not given you these words to speak?" The woman was astounded at the king's perception and cried, "Yes. He it is! O king, my master, you are exceeding wise, and nothing escapes your eyes. Truly you know whatever deeds are done upon earth."

***** *"Nothing escapes the master's eye."* *****

> **The "Mad" General**
> **("The Mule Laden with Corn and the Mule Laden with Gold"**
> **in light of I Samuel 21:10—22:1)**

A valiant general was fleeing for his life from a king who was very jealous of him. Having come to an enemy kingdom, the general hoped to find respite there from his fugitive lifestyle. But soon the servants of the enemy king became alarmed and reported to their sovereign, "Is this not the general who commands almost as a king in his own land. Do not the young girls of his land dance and sing about him, describing how he has killed tens of thousands of our people?"

When the general heard this, he became fearful for his life and made a sly plan to deceive the enemy king. Immediately **in the presence of the king and his servants, the general humbled himself and began to act insane. He wrote meaningless messages in the public court area and even allowed drool to ooze upon his beard.**

Then the king became frustrated at his servants and yelled at them, "This man is obviously mad! Why have you brought him to me? Do I need a crazy person with me to make my life better? Should I let him come and live with me in my home?" So the general was released as an "unimportant" fool, and he escaped to a cave in the wilderness.

***** *"Humble occupation is often a security."* *****

> **The Well-loved Soldier**
> **("The Fox and the Sick Lion** in light of I Samuel 18:6—20:42)

A young soldier endeared himself to a king by his valiant deeds. But soon the soldier's prowess and success caused the king to envy him. This was made worse by the love that the king's son and daughter had for the soldier. **One day, while the soldier was playing music for the king, the king took a spear and tried to murder the soldier.**

After marrying the king's daughter, the soldier again serenaded the king in his home. And just as surely, once again the king tried to spear the soldier to the wall. This time the soldier clearly saw his fate if he were to remain, so he went home to his wife, the princess, and she helped him escape.

The king continued to seek the soldier that he might slay him, but the prince also met with the soldier secretly and helped him flee the land, unbeknownst to his father the king. Thus, the soldier learned that it is not always proper to be "led" by so evil a tyrant.

***** *"Be not too easily led."* *****

> **The Lying General**
> **("The Monkey and the Dolphin" in light of I Samuel 21:1-9; 22:6-23)**

A general (popular among the people but envied by his ruler) hurriedly fled for his life from this wicked king, and escaped with a few of his loyal men to a sacred city of priests. When the head priest there saw the general with so few soldiers, he asked him why this was so.

The general answered, "I am on a top-secret mission for the king, and he commanded me to tell no one about it. I have sent my troops to their assigned places." Believing this falsehood, the priest equipped the general with a sword and fed his men.

But one of the king's servants, a vicious and evil man, was in the sacred city and reported to the king what the priest had done for the general. When brought before the king, the priest honestly said he knew nothing of the king's feud with the general (for he still believed the general's false story). In a rage, the king accused the priest and his family of deceit, and ordered the execution of all in the sacred city. Then that same evil servant of the king came and slew the priests of the city with all their families and livestock in one day. Only one son of the head priest escaped, who went, and finding the general, told him what had happened.

"I am so sorry," said the general, "for I knew that day I spoke with your father that the king's servant would betray us. I have caused the death of your entire family." So the general, whose falsehood had caused such misery and destruction to the priest's family, took the priest's son in and cared for him.

***** *"Falsehood leads to destruction."* *****

> **The Waylaid Kings**
> **("The Wild Geese and the Tame Geese" in light of Joshua 10:1-28)**

The presiding general of a young nation handily defeated a rival nation in battle. The ruler of a nearby kingdom heard of their success and decided to preempt any similar attack on his people. Summoning four other local kings, the ruler convinced them to form an alliance against their new common enemy.

Thus they met the general in battle away from their own lands, and were thoroughly routed by him. As the five kings tried to escape over unfamiliar territory, giant hailstones fell from the sky and wiped out many in their armies. Hoping to evade the general by hiding in a cave, the five kings waited within and did not return to their homes.

The general learned of their whereabouts and grabbed them from the cave.

He had his captains place their feet upon the throats of the five kings as they lay prostrate before him. "This is what will happen to all who oppose us," cried the general—he killed the kings with his sword, and then hung them on trees for all to see.

***** *"Home is always safer than strange places."* *****

> **The Evil Sorceress**
> **("The Frog Who Wished to Be as Big as an Ox"**
> **in light of I Kings 16:29-33 & II Kings 9:30-37)**

An evil sorceress married a king and bewitched him so that she in fact ruled the land. After forcing her magical spells and her hatred for all good things upon the kingdom, a young warrior rose up to destroy her evil reign.

When the warrior came to the city where she was staying, she learned of his upcoming arrival, but conceitedly thought she was greater than her foe. Putting on her finest royal wear and painting her face to impress all with her power and authority, she brazenly stood on a tower and mocked the warrior as he entered the gate of the city. "Are you not a rebel who deals falsely with his master?" she barked.

The warrior looked up and saw his foe. **"Who is on my side? Who of you is with me?" he called out to those in the tower.**

A few royal officers looked out to see the warrior. "Throw her down," he commanded. And so they did. The warrior trampled her lifeless body with his steed, and then retired to eat and drink within the castle. Later he ordered his men to bury the sorceress, but only her skull and hands and feet remained—her corpse having been eaten by dogs.

***** *"Self-conceit may lead to self-destruction."* *****

➤ The Wise Prophet and His Foes
("The Dog and the Crocodile" in light of Matthew 22:15-22)

A wise prophet spoke forth the truth, and this caused the treachery of many religious leaders to be exposed. Hoping to trap the prophet, they sent a delegation of legalistic toadies and royal sycophants to entangle him in his speech. They wanted to find evidence to accuse him of not paying his proper taxes to the imperial government.

So they began the charade, "O Master, we know that you are absolutely true and all that you teach points to genuine understanding. We also know that you have no friends when it comes to guarding your integrity, and that you place no value on any worldly position or authority. Therefore, could you tell us if it is right to give money to the emperor? Or should we not?"

But the prophet's wisdom was greater than their deceit. Seeing through their ploy, he guardedly rebuked them. **"Why do you try to trick me, you malicious play actors?**

Let me see a coin used to pay imperial tribute." So they showed him a coin. "Now," he said to them, "whose picture do you see here?" They said, "It is the emperor, and it also has his name inscribed upon it." Then the prophet replied, "Give back to the emperor what belongs to him, but do not neglect your divine duties as well!"

****** "We can never be too carefully guarded against acquaintance with persons of bad character." ******

➢ **The Obstinate Ruler**
   ("The Viper and the File" in light of Exodus 7—12**)**

A magnificent ruler oppressed a foreign nation and made them slaves in his royal city. One of these foreigners, who had previously been in exile, rose up and withstood the ruler, commanding him to free his fellow slaves. Of course, the ruler refused.

Then the exile and his brother warned the ruler that evil would befall his nation if he refused to be sensible and allow the foreigners to go free. The ruler became more and more obstinate, as indeed horrific plagues came to the ruler's land.

Eventually, the ruler's own people besought him to set the foreigners free, but his heart was hardened and would not give in. Only after the insensible ruler's own son (and the firstborn sons throughout his kingdom) had been killed by plague, did the ruler appear to relent. **But hardening his heart once again, he attacked the foreigners—and was destroyed with his army in the process.**

***** *"It is useless attacking the insensible."* *****

> **The Hapless Suitor**
> **("The Lion in Love"** in light of Genesis 34:1-29**)**

A beautiful young maiden went out to visit her friends in the country, where a rich tribal prince saw her. Being captivated by her good looks, he made wild advances toward her and had sexual relations with her. The prince, tamed by his deep love and desire, asked his father to arrange a marriage between him and the damsel. But when the young girl's father heard what had happened, he waited until his sons arrived to discuss the matter. When the brothers heard of their sister's dishonor, they became enraged—just as the prince's father arrived to make his request. The tribal leader explained how much his son longed to marry the girl, and offered her family more intermarriages, wealth, and honor. He told them that trade and commerce would be open to them throughout his lands. **Then the prince himself made his plea, offering anything that the girl's family would ask.**

Being sly and deceitful, the brothers said they would consent to the marriage only if all of the men in the leader's tribe would undergo a painful religious ritual. The prince agreed to do this, despite the great physical pain it would cause, being honorable, and deeply in love with the maiden. His father, the tribal leader, met with his people and told them that if this marriage went through as planned, they could accumulate the wealth of the damsel's people. The men agreed, hoping that future wealth would be more valuable than the immediate pain they would have to bear. And so, three days after all the men of the tribe had undergone the required ritual, and they were very sore, the damsel's brothers came to their city and killed every one of them in their helpless state! Then they captured all their wealth, along with the women and children, and took them for their own. Thus, the love-struck prince died at the hands of the family he had hoped to join by marriage.

***** *"Love can tame the wildest."* *****

➢ The Harsh and Haughty Young Ruler
("The Fox Without a Tail" in light of I Kings 12:1-19 & II Chronicles 10:1-19)

A mighty king ruled a vast empire that maintained harmony within its borders and peace throughout its surrounding lands. But he was at times a harsh tyrant who took advantage of his people. Upon his death, a prince took his father's throne, and the people approached him with a request. "Your father put a heavy burden upon us, but if you lighten that burden, we will gladly serve you."

So the young king sent them away for three days so that he could consult with his advisers. Summoning the elder statesmen who had served his father, he asked their counsel. They wisely advised that he should take heed to his subjects, serve them honorably as king, and deal with them kindly.

Not satisfied, the king met with those young men he had grown up with to find out what they thought. "Can you believe the nerve of these nobodies who order you around? Tell them that whereas your father laid a burden upon them, you will make their burden back-breaking; and as he whipped them into obedience, you will rip open their backs with the lashes that you wield!" Heady with his new royal authority, the foolish king listened to his peers and refused the wise counsel of his elders. When the people heard his rough and callous answer, they cried, "We no longer have any allegiance to your dynasty," and the kingdom of this harsh and haughty ruler was divided asunder.

***** *"Do not follow bad advice."* *****

➢ **The Murderous Messenger**
   (**"The Thief and the Innkeeper"** in light of II Kings 8:7-15)

The ruler of a nomadic kingdom grew ill, and learning that a holy prophet had come to his capital city, he sent his captain to ask the prophet if he would recover from his illness. The prophet told the captain, "You will surely tell your master that he will recover, but I have seen that he shall die."

Then the prophet stared at the captain to the point of shame, and began to weep bitterly. "Why do you cry so?" asked the captain. "Because I know that you will become king and will murder and commit horrible atrocities upon the people of my land," the prophet said. The captain rebuked the prophet, "Am I a wretched cur to do such evil?" But the prophet simply and honestly told him, "I know by divine understanding that you will be king."

When the captain returned and told his tale to his king, he indeed promised that he would recover and regain his health. But the very next day, the captain dipped a heavy cloth in water and spread it over his master's face, suffocating the life out of him. And so, as the prophet had rightly foretold, he became the new king.

***** *"Every tale is not to be believed."* *****

➢ **The Woman at the Ancient Well**
   ("The Dog and the Shadow" in light of John 4:1-42)

A**powerful prophet traveled through a remote, mountainous area and came upon an ancient well. While he rested there, a local woman came to draw water. Contrary to custom, he asked her for a drink, and she replied, "Why do you speak to me, both a woman and a foreigner to you?"**

Then he explained to her, "If you understood the divine blessing available to you, and who it is that is talking with you now, you would have asked *me* to give you a drink that is truly alive!" Still not grasping his meaning, she replied, "Sir, you don't even have anything to bring up water from this well—and it is very deep! How can you give water that is alive? Are you greater than our ancestor who bequeathed this well to our people after he and his family and livestock had been refreshed by it?"

Then the prophet returned to the true substance of what he offered, "Anyone who drinks this physical water will need to drink again, but I offer 'water' that will bubble like a spring within and brings with it eternal life!" Later, the woman (and many from her village that she brought to the prophet) realized that he was indeed their long-awaited savior and brought them what was real, far greater and more lasting than the shadowy "drinks" of this life.

***** *"Beware lest you lose the substance by grasping at the shadow."* *****

➢ The Mysterious Message
("The Knight and His Charger" in light of Daniel 1—5)

A young lad was taken captive and brought to live in the palace of a mighty emperor. He was faithfully cared for with all necessary provisions by the emperor. Because of his superior wisdom, the youth was given great honor and responsibility. As he grew to manhood, he continued to faithfully serve the emperor with wise counsel and by interpreting his dreams. On one occasion, he helped the emperor overcome a life-threatening episode.

When the emperor died, his son neglected this wise counselor and led a frivolous and licentious life with his many comrades and court sycophants. During one of his raucous wine parties, the new emperor saw a message mysteriously inscribed upon the palace wall. When none of his own wise men could explain the phenomenon, the emperor was told of his father's servant and of his abilities with the supernatural.

Summoning the neglected old man, the emperor requested an answer to the riddle of the handwriting on the wall. Much to the young ruler's chagrin, the wise counselor could still receive divine guidance—for he accurately predicted that the emperor would be dead within the day!

***** *"It is unwise to neglect a useful tool, even when not in use."* *****

> **The False "Father's Son"**
> **("The Buffoon and the Countryman"**
> in light of Matthew 27:16-26; Mark 15:7-15; Luke 23:17-25 & John 18:39,40)

Long ago, a redeemer was promised who would save the world from darkness and bring true light. The prophecy came to pass, and the promised one grew to adulthood. He spoke of his divine "Father" and was known to his followers to be the "Son of the Father."

After standing against the evil powers of his day (especially those who used their religious authority to enslave others), he was taken before a military leader to be tried with sedition. Although the charge was trumped up and false, the leader listened to the redeemer's religious accusers. **Wishing to let this innocent man go, the leader offered to invoke an annual custom that allowed him to acquit the man.**

But his religious enemies incited the crowd to ask for a murderous and rebellious villain whose name meant "son of the father." With the tide of public opinion weighing upon him, the military leader reluctantly handed the true "Son of the Father" over to his foes—and they hissed and mocked at him, then killed him on a stake. When the false "son of the father" was let go, they cheered their supposed good fortune at receiving such a scoundrel back into their fold.

***** *"Men often applaud an imitation, and hiss the real thing."* *****

➤ The Persistent Hitman
("Hercules and Pallas" in light of II Corinthians 11:16-33 & II Timothy 4:7)

A hitman for an ancient priesthood loved to capture his religious enemies and even have them killed. By an amazing twist, **he realized that he was "on the wrong side," and became an advocate for those he had attacked.**

But this brought a vicious retaliation from his former friends and masters, so that they relentlessly sought to kill him. On five separate occasions, they whipped him 39 times with lashes having bone and metal on their tips. Three times he was severely beaten with rods, and once he was pelted with stones and left for dead. He was lost at sea for more than twenty-four hours and shipwrecked three different times.

During his journeys he endured danger from floods, robbers, religious enemies, foreigners, lying "friends," and typhoons. He suffered pain and fatigue, starvation and thirst, cold and nakedness. He was mercilessly attacked in cities, rural areas, and at sea. He was even let down over the wall of a city when the governor sought his life there. Yet, he persisted and finished his responsibilities to the end of his life.

***** *"Hard blows will not keep a good man down."* *****

> **The Heroic Captain's Vow**
> **("The One-Eyed Doe" in light of Judges 11:1-40)**

A man had several legitimate sons, and one son by a prostitute. The legal heirs banished their half-brother to a far-off land, where his natural leadership and strength brought him many followers. When his brothers were threatened by war with a superior enemy, they begged for the outcast to return, and promised to make him the head of their tribe if he proved victorious over their enemy.

He consented to their terms, becoming their captain, and then boldly sent messengers to the enemy to confront their aggression. Seeing that the enemy refused to relent, this heroic captain vowed that if he could win the ensuing battle, he would dedicate the life of the first person that he saw upon his return home.

After devastating twenty of the enemy's cities and subduing them handily, the captain joyfully returned home—only to be met by his daughter, his only child! Now the head of his tribe, the captain honored his vow and dedicated his daughter to a life of religious duties, so that she bore no children and produced no heirs for her father's line.

***** *"You cannot escape your fate."* *****

> **The Prideful Prince**
> **("The Stag at the Pool"** in light of II Samuel 14:25,26; 18:1-18**)**

A young shepherd was anointed to be king over a mighty nation, where he ably served as a general and later its ruler. When one of his sons slew his brother, the king banished the murderer, yet longed for him to return someday. The prince did return with the help of one of the king's generals, and began to ingratiate himself to the people.

The prince was the most handsome man in the kingdom, flawless from head to foot, and his great pride was his hair. He grew it long and shaved it once a year—and the shavings weighed four pounds! By stealth, he won the hearts of the kingdom and overthrew his father, the king—whose love he esteemed of little value. While in exile, the elder king sent a still-loyal general to fight against his son's forces—but he gave strict instructions not to harm the prince himself. However, while fleeing in battle from his father's forces, the "upstart new king," rode his beast below a low-hanging tree. **His beautiful coiffure, which had so long been his pride and joy, became entangled in the branches so that he was left hanging there.**

The king's general heard of the rebel prince's predicament and ordered his men to kill the young man, offering them money. But they refused, reminding the general of the king's command not to harm his son. So the general cried out, "I cannot waste any more time on your talk," took three arrows, and shot them through the heart of the prince who was suspended before him. Then the general ordered ten of his loyal armorbearers to finish off the prince, and they did. And thus, the source of the prince's pride ensnared him, and the great and priceless love of his father was unable to save him.

***** *"What is worth most is often valued least."* *****

> **The Hopeful Assassins**
> **("The Lion, the Fox, and the Ass" in light of II Samuel 4:1-12)**

A ruler died in battle and his captain became the new king.

But the old ruler's son continued to hold part of the kingdom. Later, this ruler's son lost a valiant general, and the people in his part of the kingdom became afraid. Two brothers, who each led small military units, came at noon to the home of the ruler's son, treacherously pretending to be gathering food supplies. Once inside, they made their way to his bedchamber, stabbed him in the heart, and chopped off his head.

Riding all night, they came to the new king and presented him with the head of their slain master, hoping for some reward. But the new king sternly reproved them, "How could I give a reward to wicked men who have slain a righteous man in his own home on his own bed? Your blood will be required for this foul deed!" So at the new king's command, his attendants killed the two assassins, cut off their hands and feet, and hung them in public view. And the head of their fallen master, he had buried in the sepulcher of the valiant general who had once served him.

***** *"Rewards are never gained by treachery."* *****

> **The Amazed Deputy**
> **("The Wolf in Sheep's Clothing"** in light of Acts 13:4-12**)**

Two ministers (and their young helper) visited an island where one of them had been raised, that they might teach others about divine truth. Hoping to help the deputy of the island in this way, they sought an audience with him.

In attendance was a pseudo-prophet who had an impeccable religious background, but who was secretly a sorcerer of the black arts. This false cloak of righteous goodness had for some time deceived the deputy and had given the sorcerer access to his affairs. So when the two ministers began to set the deputy free from such evil, the sorcerer withstood them and tried to prevent the deputy from receiving the truth. Then, one of the ministers cried, "You who are full of sly malice, a child of evil, an enemy to all good things—will you not cease to twist those things that are right?" With that, he foretold that the sorcerer would be blinded and unable to see the sun for some time.

Immediately, a dark fog fell upon the sorcerer and he wandered about seeking for someone to guide his steps. The deputy, seeing this, believed the ministers, being amazed at the true power they yielded.

***** *"Appearances are deceptive."* *****

> **Persistent Evil**
> **("The Swallow and Other Birds" in light of Exodus 17:8-16; Deuteronomy 25:17-19; Judges 3:13; I Samuel 15:1-33 & Esther 3—7)**

An evil tribe attacked a young nation that was moving to their new home. As the nation's three leaders looked on, their army defeated the foe. After the battle, they were divinely instructed to completely wipe out this enemy nation, lest they grow up and commit future evils upon them. Later they were reminded to blot out this enemy which had nipped at their heels as they traveled to their new home. Again, years later, this evil tribe mercilessly killed members of the young nation and seized an important city.

Once the nation had chosen a king and developed a fighting army, they were in a position to finally wipe out this evil enemy. But their king allowed some of the enemy to live, even the enemy's king, so that their evil line continued. Finally, hundreds of years later, when this nation had been captured, there rose up a young maid from among them, who married the emperor of their captors. As queen, she discovered members of this wicked tribe hiding in the empire who were still bent on destroying the nation.

This they almost did, but she was able to overcome the enemy and save her people. However, if this wicked nation had been destroyed in years past as commanded, much pain and anguish would have been avoided.

***** *"Destroy the seed of evil, or it will grow up to your ruin."* *****

> **The Tyrant's Excuses**
> **("The Wolf and the Lamb" in light of Exodus 7—14)**

A cruel tyrant subjected a nation into slavery and used their labor to build his cities. When a divine spokesman commanded the tyrant to free the people, he refused time and again to do so.

Each time the spokesman powerfully displayed that the tyrant was suffering for his obstinacy, **with a variety of evils that plagued the land: the river turned to blood; frogs, gnats, and flies abounded; livestock died from disease; people were covered with sores; hail destroyed crops and locusts devoured what remained; and darkness covered the land.**

After each plague, the tyrant had a fresh excuse as to why the people should remain his slaves. Finally, the firstborn of each family died. When the tyrant saw that his own eldest son was dead, and heard the weeping of his people, he relented and let the enslaved nation go. But soon, he had another excuse to return them to captivity. Marshalling his army, he pursued them and would have destroyed the nation, had not a great sea swallowed them up—destroying the tyrant and his army.

***** *"Any excuse will serve a tyrant."* *****

> **The Over-confident Prince**
> **("The Maid and the Pail of Milk" in light of I Kings 1:1—2:25)**

A prince was well loved of his father the king, who had grown quite old and was near death. The prince was the younger brother of another prince who had died in a royal intrigue against his father. So the younger brother plotted to take the kingdom subtly (rather than by force as his brother had tried to do).

Counting the kingdom to be surely his for the taking, he prepared all the accoutrements of royalty: chariots, horsemen, and fifty loyal men to run before him. The king in his old age never questioned any of these actions, for the prince was handsome and capable. Next, the prince solicited the allegiance of his father's top general and the head priest. When they were in league with him, he over-confidently felt he could make his move for the throne. The prince threw a grandiose party for all of his princely brothers and for the entire royal court. The only ones left out were his younger brother and those loyal to him (for he knew that his father, the king, cherished his younger brother's mother as queen). The prince counted on his father acknowledging him as king, since he had set so much in motion already. But his younger brother and the queen secretly met with the king and got his royal blessing. The younger brother also swiftly held a coronation where many of the people shouted for joy. When those at the prince's party heard this, they wondered what it could be. Upon learning that the younger prince was now king, they deserted their host in fear. **The hasty prince begged his younger brother to spare his life, despite his attempt at a royal coup.**

The new king agreed, upon condition that the prince would no longer seek the throne. But when their aged father died, this still over-confident prince (counting on his ability to gain power) asked his brother, the new king, if he could marry their father's former young attendant. Seeing that he was still seeking royal power in violation of their agreement, the king had his older brother put to death.

***** *"Do not count your chickens before they are hatched."* *****

> **The Foolish Savior**
> **("The Fox and the Ass" in light of Judges 6—9)**

An obscure man from a rural area was called to deliver his people from the attack of a stronger nation. Although he doubted his calling, he continued to test it. On one occasion, he put out a wool fleece and made his decision to fight based on whether it was wet or dry the next morning. Through a series of marvelous events, he defeated the enemy and brought safety and rest to his people. After his victory in saving his people, they accordingly asked him to rule them. He foolishly replied, "No, but give me your golden jewelry, for I have use of it." The people honored his request, and gave many golden ornaments and rich garments taken from their enemies as booty.

With this wealth, he made an elegant ephod to direct their religious worship. But this finery only caused the people to turn deeper into heathenism. And this "called one" became ensnared along with his family—so that after he died, one of his sons murdered all of his own brothers in order to rule the people.

***** *"Fine clothes may disguise, but silly words will disclose a fool."* *****

> **The Curser's Reward**
> **("The Nurse and the Wolf"**
> in light of II Samuel 16:5-14; 19:16-23 & I Kings 2:8,9,36-46)

A king was forced to escape from his city, and during his departure with his loyal servants, was met by a man who bitterly cursed the king and threw stones at him. When the king's bodyguard sought to slay so vile a fiend, the king stayed them and patiently waited for future judgment. Later, when the king had regained his throne, this same "curser" came to ask for mercy, and once again, the king pardoned him for a time and waited to exact vengeance. But shortly before he was to die, the king called his son and commanded him to justly deal with the man who had shown himself an enemy by wrongfully cursing him. His son agreed, and later as the new king, he wisely commanded the "curser" to remain in the capital city where he could keep an eye on him. **"For the day you pass over the royal river out of this city, you shall surely die and your blood will be upon your own head," he declared.**

The curser replied with flattering but false words, "What you say, O lord my king, is good. Your servant will obey your command." But after three years, the curser learned that two of his servants had escaped to a foreign land. Forsaking his promise to the king, he saddled his ass and journeyed outside the royal city to retrieve them. When the king learned of this treachery, he called the curser before him, pronounced judgment on his disobedience and broken promise, and had him slain that very day.

***** *"Enemies' promises were made to be broken."* *****

➢ **The Duplicitous Prophet**
   ("The Birds, the Beasts, and the Bat"
   in light of Numbers 22—24 & Joshua 13:22)

A prophet was hired by a king to curse his enemies.

But when he tried to give a curse, a blessing came forth. This displeased the king, so he had him try again and again to curse them. However, each time, it was as though the prophet had befriended the king's enemies, for he spoke forth a blessing for them. The prophet continued to have friendly relations with the king, being motivated by his bribes.

Sometime later, the king's enemies overcame the king in battle. Although the prophet's words had benefited them in the past, they killed him along with the king with whom he was found.

***** *"He that is neither one thing nor the other has no friends."* *****

➢ **The Oracles' Advice**
   ("The Goat and the Lion" in light of I Kings 22:1-40 & II Chronicles 18:1-34)

Two kings joined in a political and military alliance. When one king was about to go to war, he gave a lavish feast for the other and his entourage and said, "Will you not go out with me to fight our common enemy and take back the city which they took from us?" His ally replied, "I am with you and so are my people and all of my military might." **"But," he said, "should we not seek divine guidance before beginning our campaign?"**

The other king agreed and called about four hundred of his oracles, all of which said, "Go up against this city and you shall prevail!" (For they all hoped such talk would advance their personal interests.) But the guest-king still had an uneasy feeling about attacking the mighty army of this foe. "Isn't there anyone else who can prophesy besides these?"

The host-king reluctantly admitted that there was one other, but that his words were often contrary to the king's wishes. "Please, let us hear him nonetheless," said his guest. So they sent a messenger to bring the lone prophet before them. During that time, both kings sat in royal array upon two thrones as the oracles continued to encourage them. Their head-oracle even put iron horns upon his head and said, "This is how you will push forward unto victory!" And all the other oracles agreed, saying, "Go up unto victory!"

Now, when the messenger had come to the lone prophet, he told him what the oracles had declared and begged him to follow suit. "I can only speak the divine truth I am given," declared the prophet. When brought before the kings and the royal court, the prophet at first mockingly repeated the words of all the oracles.

But the host-king said, "Tell me now what truth you know!" The prophet responded, "What I really see is your armies scattered as sheep who have no shepherd; let each return to his own home. Filled with frustration, the host-king cried out to his guest, "Didn't I tell you that he never has a good word for me!" But the prophet continued, "Who is trying to persuade you to undertake this hopeless quest? It is the oracles who have lies in their mouths."

At that point, the head-oracle slapped the prophet in the face and mocked him, "Which direction did that lie come from?" The true prophet pronounced judgment upon the head-oracle before all. Then the king ordered the prophet to be put back in prison with only enough food and drink to stay alive. "That will be your fate until I return in peace," said the king. As he was being taken away, the prophet boldly heralded before the entire royal court, "If you return in peace, then indeed I have spoken amiss. Take heed to what I saw all you people!" The kings did go to battle, the host-king was slain, and his guest barely escaped with his life. Sadly, the king listened to those who flattered him for their own self-interested gain, and neglected the one honest man who could have saved him.

***** *"Never accept interested advice."* *****

➤ **The Ambitious Servant**
   ("The Ass Carrying an Idol" in light of II Kings 5:15-27)

A mighty, but diseased, general was cleansed by obeying the simple command of a holy man. Wishing to show his gratitude, the general offered the holy man great wealth. But he refused, and the general departed in peace.

Shortly thereafter, a servant of the holy man ran along the road and caught up with the general as he headed home. The general came down from his chariot and said, "Is everything alright?" Then the greedy servant spoke forth a bold-faced lie, "My master, the holy man, sent me to you that I might take a wedge of silver and costly garments. I have two young men with me to carry it." **Happily, the general replied, "Have *two* wedges of silver with the garments!" and the young men carried them back.**

Taking the loot from the young men, the servant hid it in his house. When the servant returned to the holy man, his master asked, "Where are you coming from?" "Nowhere," replied the servant. But his master declared, "Was not my heart with you when you turned again to the general's chariot? Is now the time to take credit for divine healing in order to gain wealth and garments and lands and servants?" And the servant caught the same disease the general had been healed of—and so did many of his descendants.

***** *"Do not try to take credit that is due to others."* *****

> **The Pleasure-seeking King and His Noble Captain**
> **("The Flies and the Honey-Pot"** in light of II Samuel 11:1—12:25)

A king sent his armies out to battle their enemies, but he stayed in his royal city. Walking on the roof of the palace one evening, he saw a beautiful woman in a house below, bathing herself there. Smitten with desire and inquiring about her, he learned that she was married—to a very loyal and faithful army captain. So the king had her brought to him, and after lying with her, she became pregnant.

Slyly hoping to conceal his misdeeds, the king ordered his general to have the loyal captain sent home. Arriving in the royal city, the captain reported to the king, who asked for an update on the battle. The king thanked him for the report and then said, "Now go to your house and enjoy yourself." And the king sent special dainties for the captain and his wife to dine upon. But the captain did not go to his wife or house—he slept with the other palace servants.

The next day when the king learned of this, he summoned the captain to him again and said, "You have come a long distance from the battlefield, why did you not go to your home?" "How could I?" he said. "My people are in tents, my general and fellow soldiers are sleeping in open fields. Is this a time for me to eat and drink at home and lie with my wife? I will not do so!"

The king told the captain to stay one more day in the royal city, and had him join the king for dinner. The king made the captain drunk and sent him home again, but once again the captain's noble character kept him from enjoying the pleasures of the city (including his wife) when his comrades were at war.

So the king sent the captain back to his general with a note which read: "Put this captain in the most dangerous part of the battle, and then pull back your forces from him so that he is killed." The general followed the king's orders and the captain lost his life.

When the king heard of this, he married the captain's widow and cloaked his pleasure-seeking deception.

But a prophet confronted him and told him that there would be consequences for his evil deed and the pain he caused.

The king repented, but nonetheless experienced great hurt, for the child that his new wife was carrying and later brought forth, died.

***** *"Pleasure bought with pains, hurts."* *****

> **The Teacher and the Hypocrites**
> **("The Wolf and the Ass"** in light of Matthew 15:1-9)

A divine teacher was eating with his companions when a group of religious leaders began to harangue him. "Why don't your people wash their hands according to the custom that we were given by our ancestors? How can they eat in this way?"

The teacher saw through their hypocrisy and said, "And why do you break the solemn and holy law given by our ancestors? It tells us to care for and respect our parents. But you say that if people have money, they should give it to your religious fund, and by so doing neglect their duty to their parents."

"Your practices are contrary to what is holy and just and good. You hypocrites, it has been well spoken of you that you are all talk and no action! **Your mouths speak fair things, but your hearts are far from what is good.**"

***** *"Practice what you preach."* *****

> **The King and the Necromancer**
> **("The Fox and the Ape"** in light of I Samuel 28 & 31**)**

An unwise king had failed to follow the advice of a prophet, and later the prophet died. **Thinking he could contact the dead, the king found a necromancer to carry out this deed.**

The woman did impersonate the dead prophet and spoke of doom and destruction for the king and his sons.

Having fallen into this evil trap, the king ate with the woman, sealing his commitment to her evil plan. Later, the king was hit in battle by archers, and both he and his sons were slain. Thus the evil prophesied by the necromancer came to pass, and proved to be a deadly snare for the foolish ruler.

***** *"You a king, and not understand a trap!"* *****

➢ **The Conceited Leader**
   ("The Mule" in light of Esther 3 & 6)

The ruler of a vast empire promoted one of his leaders to be second in command. Expecting everyone to bow before him because of his higher status, he was greatly agitated when one of the emperor's lesser servants refused to do so. So the promoted leader, filled with anger, set up a plan to not only slay the lesser servant, but also all those who belonged to his nation.

Unbeknownst to the promoted one, the lesser servant had foiled a plot to assassinate the emperor some time before. The emperor called his second in command and asked him to devise a reward for someone who greatly benefitted the emperor. **Filled with conceit, and thinking the reward was for his service to the emperor, he recommended a lavish parade and many honors.**

But to his dismay, he found that the honor was for his foe, and that he himself would lead the horse of the lesser servant as he paraded through the city amidst shouts of praise. When the parade was ended, the promoted leader covered his head and miserably skulked home in shame.

***** *"A heavy load is a sure cure for conceit."* *****

➢ **The One-week Ruler**
   ("The Horse and the Ass" in light of I Kings 16:8-20**)**

Upon the king's death, a prince inherited the kingdom of his father. One of the captains of the army was not content with his authority and thought this a good time for a military coup—where he could become king.

One day, when the new king was drunk with wine in his steward's house, the captain carried out his conspiracy and slew him. Now king, the once "nobody" captain decided to kill all of the royal family to ensure his new political and military power. After slaying all male heirs and their friends, the captain thought his one-week reign was secure for years to come.

But when the head general of the army heard of the coup, he gathered his troops and surrounded the upstart "king." Seeing his end had come after only seven days as ruler, the new king ended his life by fire.

Thus his "golden reign" proved far more dangerous than serving a master faithfully and humbly.

***** *"Better humble security than gilded danger."* *****

> **The Notorious Prophet**
> **("The Oak and the Reeds" in light of I Kings 18 & 19)**

A prophet became famous when he bested four-hundred and fifty enemy oracles. In the contest, the prophet brought down fire from heaven to ignite his sacrifice, while all of his opponents could not raise a single spark. His notoriety increased when he slew all four-hundred and fifty in retaliation for their leading the people of the land astray. But when the queen, who supported and sponsored the slain oracles, heard of his deed, she put a bounty on the life of the prophet. **So he escaped to the wilderness to lead a life of obscurity, far from the queen's spies.**

While in the wilderness, the prophet gained insight as to how he was to safely conduct his life and whom he should name his successor. Although he was no longer in the "limelight," the prophet enjoyed safety and rest.

***** *"Obscurity often brings safety."* *****

> **The Treacherous General**
> **("The Fox and the Stork"** in light of II Samuel 2—3; 20:1-13 & I Kings 2:1-34)

A noble and virtuous king named an able soldier to be general over all his host. When the kingdom became divided, the general led the king's forces against the rebels. The general's brother tried to kill the rebel captain, but was slain in the attempt. The general wanted to kill the rebel captain, but waited patiently for the opportunity to pay him back for his brother's death.

The rebel captain decided to return his allegiance to the king, and visited the king—who agreed to take back the captain and his army. But still intent upon revenge, the general called for a secret meeting with the captain and murdered him deceitfully.

Later, when the king planned to replace the general with one of the king's own relatives, the general also tricked that soldier into meeting with him—and he murdered him. So the king waited patiently until his son succeeded him as king. He told his son that once he was dead, he should exact vengeance upon the general for his cruel deeds. After the death of the king, his son (who now reigned as king) caught the treacherous general in an attempted coup against him. The general ran to the temple for protection, but the young king followed his father's wishes and had the general slain despite his "religious" appeals for mercy.

***** *"As ye sow, so shall ye reap."* *****

> **The Evil King's Advice**
> **("The Two Rats" in light of Matthew 2:1-12)**

A guild of ancient astronomers had been carefully watching the heavens for hundreds of years for a promised sign that a king would be born in a foreign land—and this king would save all mankind! When they recognized the sign in the night sky, they immediately traveled to that land and visited the royal palace.

The reigning monarch was a vicious and evil king who only thought of keeping his wealth and power. Hoping to trick the astronomers into revealing when the new "king" was born, he learned that the child was about a year and six months in age. Then the king asked his scholars where such a promised savior should be born. They told him that an ancient seer said he would be born in a nearby village. The evil king plotted to give the astronomers "advice" about what to do, hoping to be shown a way to kill the child and secure his throne. So he sent the astronomers to find the child, promising that he too would "worship" the boy once they located him. The astronomers found the young boy, worshipped him, but were divinely warned not to return and tell the king where the child was.

When the king learned his intrigue had been foiled, he sent soldiers to the village, and they killed every boy there less than two years in age. The savior-king escaped with his family, and sometime later the evil king died of a horrid disease.

***** *"Interested advisers usually are seeking some gift."* *****

> **The Honest Prophet**
> **("The Owl and the Nightingale"** in light of Matthew 23:1-12)

A wise prophet encountered his religious foes on a daily basis, and saw their egotistical attempts to control the common people.

One day he honestly revealed to a large crowd how evil these self-important tyrants were.

"They put heavy burdens on others and will not raise a finger to help anyone. They make a pretentious show in how they dress, and they always have the finest seats at any banquet and the most respected positions at their religious services. They love to have the common people approach them in public and call them 'master.' But they are hypocritical play actors, and know nothing of true service or greatness."

***** *"Self-importance means little to the truly wise."* *****

> **The Longsuffering Uncle**
> (**"The Discontented Ass" in light of Genesis 13—19**)

A young man was cared for by his uncle, who brought him with him to a new home that held great promise. The nephew and his workers were not content with their lot, but complained openly.

So, the uncle graciously gave his nephew the pick of the land, and he chose a beautiful area—that was inhabited by a wicked and perverted people.

As the unhappy nephew became inundated with the perversion of his neighbors, he tried on one occasion to prevent their wicked deeds. But they in their insolent pride, railed on him with their vicious words. Then they turned on him and tried to sexually molest and kill him and the guests in his home. The longsuffering uncle rescued his nephew from death on more than one occasion. But the unsatisfied nephew continued to see his life grow worse and worse as he tried each new way to "improve his lot."

***** *"To be unhappy, complain about your lot."* *****

➢ **The King's Servant**
   ("The Wolf and the Mastiff" in light of Ezra 9:8,9 & Nehemiah 1—6)

A noble people were conquered by a mighty kingdom and enslaved in a foreign land. Although their lot was a good one, they longed for their former freedom, even if it meant a life of difficulty. One of these slaves became servant to the king and was given permission to return to his native land and rebuild the capital city, which had fallen into ruins.

Once there, he set about organizing work crews and the project began in earnest. But enemies who lived nearby, plotted against the renovation, for they feared that this noble people would once again become strong. Thus, **the king's servant banded his workers together and gave them weapons—in one hand they held a construction tool and in the other hand a spear or sword.**

And so, working from sun up to sun down, they completed the outer protective wall in less than two months. When the leader of their local enemies heard of this, he was greatly dismayed. But the king's servant and those of his noble nation revived, and though their life included hardships, they kept their freedom for some time back in their native land.

***** *"Better starve free, than be a fat slave."* *****

> **The Promoted Youth**
> (**"The Cobbler Turned Doctor"** in light of Judges 17 & 18)

During the time when there was no king or any just ruler, everyone made their own laws. One man inherited a large sum of silver from his mother and, because he was a very religious person, used some of the silver to make an idol to go into his "house of gods." He also made one of his sons a "priest" and gave him a special chest plate for the religious services. One day, a youth from a long line of priests happened to pass the religious man's house. **Accepting the offer of silver, garments, and daily food, the youth replaced the man's son as his "priest."**

At the same time, a large tribe that was relocating to a new area heard about the house of gods, and spent the night there in their journey. Some of the tribe recognized the youth and asked what he was doing. He replied, "This man hired me, and promoted me to be his priest." The tribe asked the youth if their way would be prosperous, and even though he knew little of what he was doing, he gave the tribe assurances that all would be fine. Thinking the youth to be a boon to them, they stole him, the chest plate, and some idols from the house of gods. Finding a place where they wished to settle, the tribe killed the local inhabitants, and set up their newly-stolen "priest" to make more predictions. Thus, a boy who knew little of life was promoted to guide a whole tribe in their murderous onslaughts.

***** *"A cobbler should stick to his last."* *****

- **The Childless Queen**
  ("The Owl and the Grasshopper"
  in light of II Samuel 6:16-23 & I Chronicles 15:27-29)

A valiant and just king was married to the daughter of the former king—a man who had mercilessly tried to kill him. Forgiving her father's transgressions, he loved his queen and cared for her.

One day, to celebrate a religious victory, the king danced before the rejoicing crowds with fervor and abandon.

Thinking this unbecoming of her "royal" husband, the queen flattered him with false admiration. "How glorious was the king on this special day," she said, "when he removed his regal garments and paraded about as happy as a commoner!"

Seeing through her sarcasm, the king had enough. He allowed her to remain queen, but never loved her again to the end that she bore him children.

***** *Flattery is not a proof of true admiration.* *****

> **The Outspoken Leader**
> **("The Swallow and the Crow"** in light of Matthew 26:30-35,69-75)

A long-awaited prophet, who came to bring salvation to his people, gathered a small band of leaders to help him in his mission. The most outspoken of the group became a constant companion and earned the prophet's favor for his strength and commitment.

But one day, the prophet accurately foretold that all of his band would desert him for a time. The outspoken leader denied such a claim, and promised profusely to never leave his master's side.

Then the prophet spoke again, **"I tell you assuredly, before the early morning hours come, you will three times deny that you even know me."**

"What! I would die before disowning you," the leader professed.

But that same night, when the prophet was captured by his enemies to be killed, and the outspoken leader faced a similar fate, he swore that he had never heard of the prophet.

***** *"Fine-weather friends are not worth much."* *****

> **The Hidden Prophet**
> **("The Town Mouse and the Country Mouse"** in light of I Kings 17:1-16)

A wise and fearless prophet foretold to the king that a severe drought (lasting for years) would soon begin in the land.

Since the queen hated the prophet and sought to kill him, he escaped to the wilderness—where he found food placed in the rocks by birds and drank from a clean brook.

When the brook dried up, the prophet was guided to stay with a widow and her son, well hidden from the queen's intrigue. Although his food was simple, it was never lacking during his time there.

Later, the prophet (who never bowed in fear to the queen to receive her favor or fancy treats) was once again nourished when he again escaped to the wilderness.

***** *"Better beans and bacon in peace, than cakes and ale in fear."* *****

> **The Fear-filled King**
> **("The Lion, the Fox, and the Wolf"** in light of I Samuel 15-31**)**

A young man, who thought little of himself and feared he would fail, was chosen to be king because of his great height and strength. Yet his integrity was lacking, so that he made serious blunders that should have cost him his crown.

Fearing that one of his generals (who was a much better man than he in all ways) would usurp the throne, he ruthlessly attacked him and hunted him down. **This so consumed the king that he became embroiled in dangerous battles.**

Prior to one fight, the king sought the advice of a witch to find out his future. Once again, the king fell into the snare of fear, jealousy, and hatred—for the witch excelled in such evil. She talked him into eating with her and forming an alliance. Then she filled him with even more fear and "prophesied" of his death in battle the next day. Now wholly taken with fear, he succumbed to her vile words and the very next day was slain in a skirmish.

***** "It is easier to get into the enemy's toils than out again." *****

> ### The Courageous Savior
> ("The King's Son and the Painted Lion" in light of Matthew 26:36-46)

A promised savior fulfilled his service with humility and love. When it came time for him to die a horrible and painful death (as had been foretold by many ancient seers), he sought divine guidance to find some other method to complete his mission.

He even enlisted the help of friends to support him during this dark hour, but they fell asleep from sorrow.

Finally, after three requests for guidance to alter the course before him, he learned that such a horrific sacrifice was the only way to achieve his ends.

Summoning more courage than any other at any time, he walked forward to bear his cross and bravely accomplished his charge.

***** *"We had better bear our troubles bravely than try to escape them."* *****

> **The Wise Woman**
> **("The Mice in Council"** in light of II Samuel 20:1-22**)**

After squelching a rebellion led by his own son, a ruler returned to his palace. But soon thereafter, a cowardly dissenter gathered together part of the kingdom and led them away in defiance of the king. Seeing that this latest desertion could do more harm than his son's rebellion, the king sent out a trusted general and his troops after the dissenter to dispatch him before he could find refuge in a secure city. Having pursued the dissenter, they trapped him and besieged the town where he dwelt. The troops cast a mound near the wall of the city within a trench, and then began to pound the city gates with battering rams.

Things looked bleak for the inhabitants of the city in this "impossible" situation, and few sound remedies were offered from them. But one wise woman came up with a plan, and asked the general for a truce and parley. The general agreed to meet her, and the woman asked if he would consider her proposed bargain. "I am listening," he said. The wise woman continued, "There is an old saying that our town is where problems cease and questions are answered. Yet your army threatens to kill me and all those within our gates. Why do you such a thing?" The general explained that he only wanted the dissenter who withstood the king. He told her that he was hiding within her town and that if she would turn him over, the general and his army would depart in peace.

The woman gave this promise, "His head will be thrown to you over the wall!" She wisely met with the leaders of her city and they agreed to her remedy. True to her word, the dissenter's head was tossed to the general, bringing peace to the town.

***** *"It is easy to propose impossible remedies."* *****

- **The Kangaroo Court**
  ("The Hare Afraid of His Ears" in light of Matthew 26:57-68 & Mark 14:53-65)

A kind and faithful teacher often resorted to a magnificent temple to bring understanding to those who would go there. **Becoming jealous of his following, temple leaders plotted to kill the teacher.**

Hoping to use his own words against him, they sent out spies to take note of his teachings and report back to them. Although they sought many false witnesses, none could agree and thus were useless in legal proceedings against the teacher.

Finally, the head temple leader arrested the teacher on false charges and brought him before their council. He presented the disagreeing testimonies of his "witnesses" to the teacher, who wisely remained silent during this kangaroo court. When nothing else could be found to accuse the teacher of, he asked the teacher of his credentials. The teacher boldly proclaimed that he was the chosen teacher for the people, and that the temple leader would one day be forced to acknowledge it. Filled with rage, the temple leader pronounced a guilty sentence, and the council dutifully agreed. Then they spat on the teacher, reviled him, and sent him away to be executed.

***** *"Your enemies will use any excuse to attack you."* *****

The Uncivil Ruler
("The Mastiff and the Goose" in light of II Samuel 10:1-19 & I Chronicles 19:1-19)

A king heard that a friendly ruler in a neighboring land had died, so he sent royal ambassadors to offer condolences to the ruler's family. **"I will show kindness to the ruler's son, for his father showed kindness to me," the king declared.**

But now that the son reigned in his father's stead, he listened to the princes of the land who said: "Do you think this king is really honoring your dead father? Is he not sending these so-called ambassadors to spy out our land so that he may overthrow us with his armies?"

Taking this false admonition to heart, the young ruler disgraced the ambassadors by shaving their beards (for beards were considered a sacred thing) and cutting off their garments so that their buttocks were visible. The ambassadors left in disgrace, and when the king learned of this uncivilized treatment, he personally found the ambassadors and comforted them, for they were filled with shame. He graciously allowed them to stay in a nearby city and return to the palace later when their beards were grown back. When the young ruler and his supporters saw that they were now odious to the king, they hired mercenaries to fight the king. But the king's forces were much greater in number and better fighters than the young ruler and his mercenaries. Handily defeated, the mercenaries left the field and vowed never to help the young ruler again. Thus, the young ruler was overcome by a great enemy, who could have been his friend if he had only treated him civilly.

***** *"Sure, those who have neither strength nor weapons to fight at least should be civil."* *****

> **The Sorcerer's Repentance**
> **("The Sorceress" in light of Acts 8:9-24)**

A sorcerer used his magical arts to bewitch an entire city and convinced them that he was a "great one." Everyone in the city gave heed to his charms, from the least to the greatest, professing that he was "The Great Power of God"! This continued for a long time as the sorcerer worked his magic upon them.

But one day, a truly powerful speaker came to the city and taught the people of genuine power. **His words were backed up with magnificent works—so that even the sorcerer sought this new and powerful truth.**

But the sorcerer's heart was still not pure. He hoped to use this truth to once more control the people. Not sure how to handle the sorcerer, the speaker sent for two of his wise friends, who came to the city. Once there, one of the speaker's friends confronted the sorcerer for his lack of judgment and told him that this power was only to be used for good, and not for evil. Seeing his heart laid bare by words of truth, the sorcerer repented of his evil intent and asked that nothing evil come upon him for his past misdeeds.

***** *"Use your given powers with judgment."* *****

> **The King's Burdens**
> **("The Lion, the Ass, and the Fox" in light of I Samuel 8:10-22)**

A people requested from their holy man that a king might rule them, hoping for security and prosperity within their lands. He honestly and carefully told them what a burden the king's rule would be:

"He will take your sons to be his charioteers and footmen, to fill his army of thousands of soldiers, to plant his fields and reap his harvest, and to make his implements of war. He will also take your daughters to be his perfumers, his cooks, and bakers. He will steal the best of your fields and vineyards and olive yards so that he may give them as rewards to his loyal supporters. He will force a tribute of one tenth of your crops and grapes to feed his officers and servants. He will take the best of your employees and your finest youths (and even your work animals) to do his work for him. He will take a tenth of your sheep, and you will become his slaves!"

But the warning fell on deaf ears, for the people had their king. Only later did they see that their work had increased, but the reward of their labor had waned.

***** *"You may share the labors of the great, but you will not share the spoil."* *****

> **The Enlightened Apprentice**
> **("The Fly and the Draught-Mule" in light of Acts 9:1-22)**

A young man apprenticed himself to the top religious leaders of his nation and served them as his masters. That same nation had a promised hero who had built a group of followers that carried on his message, winning many others. When the religious leaders became opposed to these followers, they sent out their young apprentice to capture and kill those in the group.

While on the road to carry out such a mission, the apprentice encountered the hero in a glorified form. Stunned by his majesty, the apprentice asked him who he was, and the hero explained that he was the true master.

Forsaking his religious handlers, the apprentice changed the course of his life and began to tell others about the hero. He became more enlightened about his new master's truth and later helped many thousands find true happiness through what the hero had to offer.

***** *"Everyone should know his Master."* *****

> **The Clever Captive**
> **("The Satyr and the Traveler"** in light of Acts 23:1-10)

A man was captured by his religious foes and brought before them. He had been known to promote a way of life that this group of religious leaders opposed. But part of the group held one set of beliefs regarding spiritual matters and the other held a worldly and five-senses approach to life. Their leaders hoped to speak against this man from both sides.

When the captive discerned this division among their ranks, he cleverly used it to his advantage. "I was raised to follow the beliefs of the spiritual group here, as did my father. It is for these spiritual beliefs that I am called in question." This aroused support from the spiritual group and awoke the ire of those who went more by their five senses. Neither side could fully trust the other.

A bitter quarrel began between the two factions, with heated words and violent action—so that the local government authorities stepped in and rescued the captive from the evil intent of his foes.

***** *"The man who talks for both sides is not to be trusted."* *****

➢ The Vain Bewitcher
("The Eagle and the Crow" in light of Acts 8:9-24)

A sorcerer used cunning arts to bewitch the people in his home area. He carried out his deceitful craft for many days so that the local populace called him the "Great Power of God." Accepting their adulation, the sorcerer greatly overestimated his real powers.

One day, a man with greater power arrived and the people began to follow him. **Filled with vanity and convinced that he too could wield such power, the sorcerer offered to buy this ability.**

But that proved to be his undoing, for this greater power could only be used for good and not witchcraft. Being confronted for his evil thinking, the sorcerer was forced to realize that only with proper motive can great power be truly used.

***** *"Do not let your vanity make you overestimate your powers."* *****

> **The Lying Thief**
> **("The Shepherd Boy and the Wolf"**
> **in light of Matthew 26:14-16; 27:3-5 & John 12:6)**

There was a holy man who assembled a group of twelve protégées. One of these was given control over the finances for the group, but he was a thief and stole what was in their common fund.

Later, when bribed by religious and political leaders, he promised to hand over the holy man (who he personally knew had only done good to others) in exchange for money. Once the bargain was made and the holy man was taken, the thief decided to try and convince his bribers that the holy man was not worthy of their hatred and vicious treatment. **"I have betrayed an innocent man to you!" he truly cried.**

But his pleas fell on deaf ears, for they cared not for this lying thief, and were hell-bent on destroying his wise and holy master.

***** *"A liar will not be believed, even when he speaks the truth."* *****

> **The Foolishly Greedy Rich Man**
> **("The Wolf and the Crane" in light of I Samuel 25:1-42)**

A rich man had three thousand sheep and a thousand goats, and was shearing them. A noble leader of a group of outcasts learned about the shearing and sent a message to the rich man:

"Peace be to you, to all in your house, and to all that you own. We have heard you are shearing the very sheep that we have protected with our lives for many days. Ask your young shepherds and they will verify that we kept them from danger in the wild. **Now we ask for your gracious favor and any share of your abundance that you would care to give us in gratitude for our assistance, dear father.**"

But hearing this kind entreaty, the foolishly greedy rich man retorted: "Who is this vagabond that is an outcast from the king? He is but one of many who have betrayed their masters. Should I take of my bread and water and food that are prepared for my shearers, and give it to him?" The messengers returned with the rich man's rude answer, and the outcast leader was livid at such ingratitude. Were it not for the rich man's wife and her kind intervention, the leader would have slain the rich man. And in truth, he died a short time later when he learned how close of a brush with death he had at the hand of the one he had insulted.

***** *"Gratitude and greed go not together."* *****

> **The Crushed Conqueror**
> ("The Gnat and the Lion" in light of Judges 9:22-57)

A wicked prince bribed his relatives to support him in taking the crown, and later killed all but one of his many brothers to secure his power. After reigning as king for three years, others rebelled against him and waged open war. The king routed the rebels in battle, and then besieged them in a tower to which they had escaped.

Thinking that he could once more use his cunning to overcome his foes, he commanded his forces to gather wood and build a fire to burn down the tower—and all within it were killed.

Later, he besieged another city with a tower, into which the men and women of that area had fled. Confident that his plan would work once again, he brought wood near the base of the tower. But a woman saw him from above and dropped a large milling stone upon his head, crushing his skull. He called for his young armorbearer and said, "Draw your sword and slay me, for let it not be said that I was killed by a woman!" The young man obeyed and swiftly dispatched the king. Thus, the conqueror of great armies was done in by the least of his enemies.

***** *"The least of our enemies is often the most to be feared."* *****

Appendix—Morals from Aesop Found in the Book of Proverbs

"Biggest is not always best."

Proverbs 15:16:
Better *is* little with the fear of the Lord than great treasure and trouble therewith.

Proverbs16:8:
Better *is* a little with righteousness than great revenues without right.

"Little friends may prove great friends."

Proverbs 30:24-28:
There be four *things which are* little upon the earth, but they *are* exceeding wise:
The ants *are* a people not strong, yet they prepare their meat in the summer;
The conies *are but* a feeble folk, yet make they their houses in the rocks;
The locusts have no king, yet go they forth all of them by bands;
The spider taketh hold with her hands, and is in kings' palaces.

"Greed often costs more than one could imagine."

Proverbs 1:19:
So *are* the ways of every one that is greedy of gain; *which* taketh away the life of the owners thereof.

Proverbs 15:27:
He that is greedy of gain troubleth his own house; but he that hateth gifts shall live.

"Be careful of the company you keep."

Proverbs 13:20:
He that walketh with wise *men* shall be wise: but a companion of fools shall be destroyed.

Proverbs 28:7,24:
Whoso keepeth the law *is* a wise son: but he that is a companion of riotous *men* shameth his father.
Whoso robbeth his father or his mother, and saith, *It is* no transgression; the same *is* the companion of a destroyer.

Proverbs 29:3,24:
Whoso loveth wisdom rejoiceth his father: but he that keepeth company with harlots spendeth *his* substance.
Whoso is partner with a thief hateth his own soul: he heareth cursing, and bewrayeth *it* not.

"The flatterer robs by stealth, taking from his victim both wisdom and wealth."

Proverbs 2:16:
To deliver thee from the strange woman, *even* from the stranger *which* flattereth with her words.

Proverbs 6:24:
To keep thee from the evil woman, from the flattery of the tongue of a strange woman.

Proverbs 7:5,21:
That they may keep thee from the strange woman, from the stranger *which* flattereth with her words. With her much fair speech she caused him to yield, with the flattering of her lips she forced him.

Proverbs 20:19:
He that goeth about *as* a talebearer revealeth secrets: therefore meddle not with him that flattereth with his lips.

Proverbs 26:28:
A lying tongue hateth *those that are* afflicted by it; and a flattering mouth worketh ruin.

Proverbs 28:23:
He that rebuketh a man afterwards shall find more favour than he that flattereth with the tongue.

Proverbs 29:5:
A man that flattereth his neighbour spreadeth a net for his feet.

"Contentment is the first law of happiness."

Proverbs 30:8,9:
Remove far from me vanity and lies: give me neither poverty nor riches; feed me with food convenient for me:
Lest I be full, and deny *thee,* and say, Who *is* the Lord? or lest I be poor, and steal, and take the name of my God *in vain.*

"A little correct action today is worth countless attempts at righting things in the future."

Proverbs 5:7:
Hear me now therefore, O ye children, and depart not from the words of my mouth.

Proverbs 6:3:
Do this now, my son, and deliver thyself, when thou art come into the hand of thy friend; go, humble thyself, and make sure thy friend.

Proverbs 7:24:
Hearken unto me now therefore, O ye children, and attend to the words of my mouth.

Proverbs 8:32:
Now therefore hearken unto me, O ye children: for blessed *are they that* keep my ways.

"The loiterer often imputes delay to his more active friend."

Proverbs 6:6:
Go to the ant, thou sluggard; consider her ways, and be wise.

Proverbs 6:9:
How long wilt thou sleep, O sluggard? when wilt thou arise out of thy sleep?

Proverbs 10:26:
As vinegar to the teeth, and as smoke to the eyes, so *is* the sluggard to them that send him.

Proverbs 13:4:
The soul of the sluggard desireth, and *hath* nothing: but the soul of the diligent shall be made fat.

Proverbs 20:4:
The sluggard will not plow by reason of the cold; *therefore* shall he beg in harvest, and have nothing.

Proverbs 26:16:
The sluggard *is* wiser in his own conceit than seven men that can render a reason.

"Better one safe way than a hundred on which you cannot depend."

Proverbs 1:33:
But whoso hearkeneth unto me shall dwell safely, and shall be quiet from fear of evil.

Proverbs 3:23:
Then shalt thou walk in thy way safely, and thy foot shall not stumble.

Proverbs 11:14:
Where no counsel is, the people fall: but in the multitude of counsellors there is safety.

Proverbs 18:10:
The name of the Lord is a strong tower: the righteous runneth into it, and is safe.

Proverbs 21:31:
The horse is prepared against the day of battle: but safety is of the Lord.

Proverbs 24:6:
For by wise counsel thou shalt make thy war: and in multitude of counsellors there is safety.

Proverbs 29:25:
The fear of man bringeth a snare: but whoso putteth his trust in the Lord shall be safe.

Proverbs 31:11:
The heart of her husband doth safely trust in her, so that he shall have no need of spoil.

"One good turn deserves another."

Proverbs 11:25:
The liberal soul shall be made fat: and he that watereth shall be watered also himself.

Proverbs 13:21:
Evil pursueth sinners: but to the righteous good shall be repayed.

Proverbs 19:17:
He that hath pity upon the poor lendeth unto the Lord; and that which he hath given will he pay him again.

"Outside show is a poor substitute for inner worth."

Proverbs 11:22:
As a jewel of gold in a swine's snout, *so is* a fair woman which is without discretion.

Proverbs 31:30:
Favour *is* deceitful, and beauty *is* vain: *but* a woman *that* feareth the Lord, she shall be praised.

"To give well one must give wisely."

Proverbs 3:28:
Say not unto thy neighbour, Go, and come again, and to morrow I will give; when thou hast it by thee.

Proverbs 9:9:
Give *instruction* to a wise *man,* and he will be yet wiser: teach a just *man,* and he will increase in learning.

Proverbs 11:30:
The fruit of the righteous *is* a tree of life; and he that winneth souls *is* wise.

Proverbs 13:15:
Good understanding giveth favour: but the way of transgressors *is* hard.

Proverbs 16:20:
He that handleth a matter wisely shall find good: and whoso trusteth in the Lord, happy *is* he.

Proverbs 19:17:
He that hath pity upon the poor lendeth unto the Lord; and that which he hath given will he pay him again.

Proverbs 22:9:
He that hath a bountiful eye shall be blessed; for he giveth of his bread to the poor.

Proverbs 31:15:
She riseth also while it is yet night, and giveth meat to her household, and a portion to her maidens.

"Never trust a friend who deserts you in time of need."

Proverbs 10:26:
As vinegar to the teeth, and as smoke to the eyes, so *is* the sluggard to them that send him.

Proverbs 13:17:
A wicked messenger falleth into mischief: but a faithful ambassador *is* health.

Proverbs 25:19:
Confidence in an unfaithful man in time of trouble *is like* a broken tooth, and a foot out of joint.

"United we stand, divided we fall."

Proverbs 12:7:
The wicked are overthrown, and *are* not: but the house of the righteous shall stand.

Proverbs 14:4:
Where no oxen *are,* the crib *is* clean: but much increase *is* by the strength of the ox.

Proverbs 17:1:
Better *is* a dry morsel, and quietness therewith, than an house full of sacrifices *with* strife.

"Look before you leap."

Proverbs 14:29:
He that is slow to wrath *is* of great understanding: but *he that is* hasty of spirit exalteth folly.

Proverbs 19:2:
Also, *that* the soul *be* without knowledge, *it is* not good; and he that hasteth with *his* feet sinneth.

Proverbs 21:5:
The thoughts of the diligent *tend* only to plenteousness; but of every one *that is* hasty only to want.

Proverbs 28:22:
He that hasteth to be rich *hath* an evil eye, and considereth not that poverty shall come upon him.

Proverbs 29:20:
Seest thou a man *that is* hasty in his words? *there is* more hope of a fool than of him.

"You will only injure yourself if you take notice of despicable enemies."

Proverbs 27:6:
Faithful *are* the wounds of a friend; but the kisses of an enemy *are* deceitful.

"Little by little does the trick."

Proverbs 10:4:
He becometh poor that dealeth *with* a slack hand: but the hand of the diligent maketh rich.

Proverbs 22:19:
That thy trust may be in the Lord, I have made known to thee this day, even to thee.

"Handsome is as handsome does."

Proverbs 20:11:
Even a child is known by his doings, whether his work *be* pure, and whether *it be* right.

"Be content with your lot."

Proverbs 13:25:
The righteous eateth to the satisfying of his soul: but the belly of the wicked shall want.

Proverbs 27:20:
Hell and destruction are never full; so the eyes of man are never satisfied.

"It was a poor rule that does not work both ways."

Proverbs 11:1:
A false balance *is* abomination to the Lord: but a just weight *is* his delight.

Proverbs 16:11:
A just weight and balance *are* the Lord's: all the weights of the bag *are* his work.

Proverbs 20:23:
Divers weights *are* an abomination unto the Lord; and a false balance *is* not good.

"We often give our enemies the means for our own destruction."

Proverbs 6:32:
But whoso committeth adultery with a woman lacketh understanding: he *that* doeth it destroyeth his own soul.

Proverbs 10: 29:
The way of the Lord *is* strength to the upright: but destruction *shall be* to the workers of iniquity.

Proverbs 11:3:
The integrity of the upright shall guide them: but the perverseness of transgressors shall destroy them.

Proverbs 13:20:
He that walketh with wise *men* shall be wise: but a companion of fools shall be destroyed.

Proverbs 21:15:
It is joy to the just to do judgment: but destruction *shall be* to the workers of iniquity.

Proverbs 24:2:
For their heart studieth destruction, and their lips talk of mischief.

Proverbs 28:24:
Whoso robbeth his father or his mother, and saith, *It is* no transgression; the same *is* the companion of a destroyer.

"It is best to prepare for the days of necessity."

Proverbs 16:1:
The preparations of the heart in man, and the answer of the tongue, *is* from the Lord.

Proverbs 21:31:
The horse is prepared against the day of battle: but safety *is* of the Lord.

Proverbs 24:27:
Prepare thy work without, and make it fit for thyself in the field; and afterwards build thine house.

Proverbs 30:25:
The ants *are* a people not strong, yet they prepare their meat in the summer.

"Borrow not to fool others."

Proverbs 22:7:
The rich ruleth over the poor, and the borrower *is* servant to the lender.

"It is hard for a rogue to establish his innocence at any time."

Proverbs 6:29:
So he that goeth in to his neighbour's wife; whosoever toucheth her shall not be innocent.

Proverbs 19:29:
Judgments are prepared for scorners, and stripes for the back of fools.

Proverbs 28:20:
A faithful man shall abound with blessings: but he that maketh haste to be rich shall not be innocent.

"Selfishness brings its own pains."

Proverbs 3:5,7:
Trust in the Lord with all thine heart; and lean not unto thine own understanding.
Be not wise in thine own eyes: fear the Lord, and depart from evil.

Proverbs 18:17:
He that is first in his own cause *seemeth* just; but his neighbour cometh and searcheth him.

Proverbs 20:6:
Most men will proclaim every one his own goodness: but a faithful man who can find?

Proverbs 25:6,7,27:
Put not forth thyself in the presence of the king, and stand not in the place of great *men:*
For better *it is* that it be said unto thee, Come up hither; than that thou shouldest be put lower in the presence of the prince whom thine eyes have seen.
It is not good to eat much honey: so *for men* to search their own glory *is not* glory.

"Self-help is usually the best help."

Proverbs 5:15,17:
Drink waters out of thine own cistern, and running waters out of thine own well.
Let them be only thine own, and not strangers' with thee.

"False promises bring their own punishment."

Proverbs 19:5,9:
A false witness shall not be unpunished, and *he that* speaketh lies shall not escape.
A false witness shall not be unpunished, and *he that* speaketh lies shall perish.

"Time well spent is not wasted."

Proverbs 9:10,11:
The fear of the Lord *is* the beginning of wisdom: and the knowledge of the holy *is* understanding.
For by me thy days shall be multiplied, and the years of thy life shall be increased.

Proverbs 16:20:
He that handleth a matter wisely shall find good: and whoso trusteth in the Lord, happy *is* he.

Proverbs 21:12:
The righteous *man* wisely considereth the house of the wicked: *but God* overthroweth the wicked for *their* wickedness.

Proverbs 28:26:
He that trusteth in his own heart is a fool: but whoso walketh wisely, he shall be delivered.

"Cunning often outwits itself."

Proverbs 3:7:
Be not wise in thine own eyes: fear the Lord, and depart from evil.

Proverbs 12:15:
The way of a fool *is* right in his own eyes: but he that hearkeneth unto counsel *is* wise.

Proverbs 16:2:
All the ways of a man *are* clean in his own eyes; but the Lord weigheth the spirits.

Proverbs 18:11:
The rich man's wealth *is* his strong city, and as an high wall in his own conceit.

Proverbs 21:2
Every way of a man *is* right in his own eyes: but the Lord pondereth the hearts.

Proverbs 26:12,16:
Seest thou a man wise in his own conceit? *there is* more hope of a fool than of him.
The sluggard *is* wiser in his own conceit than seven men that can render a reason.

Proverbs 28:11:
The rich man *is* wise in his own conceit; but the poor that hath understanding searcheth him out.

Proverbs 30:12:
There is a generation *that are* pure in their own eyes, and *yet* is not washed from their filthiness.

"It is easy to judge your true friends by the amount of care they exercise for your welfare."

Proverbs 17:17:
A friend loveth at all times, and a brother is born for adversity.

Proverbs 18:24:
A man *that hath* friends must shew himself friendly: and there is a friend *that* sticketh closer than a brother.

Proverbs 27:6,10,17:
Faithful *are* the wounds of a friend; but the kisses of an enemy *are* deceitful.
Thine own friend, and thy father's friend, forsake not; neither go into thy brother's house in the day of thy calamity: *for* better *is* a neighbour *that is* near than a brother far off.
Iron sharpeneth iron; so a man sharpeneth the countenance of his friend.

"The weak often revenge themselves on those who use them ill, even though they be more powerful."

Proverbs 6:3:
Do this now, my son, and deliver thyself, when thou art come into the hand of thy friend; go, humble thyself, and make sure thy friend.

Proverbs 11:27:
He that diligently seeketh good procureth favour: but he that seeketh mischief, it shall come unto him.

"Not to help others has no rewards."

Proverbs 3:27-30:
Withhold not good from them to whom it is due, when it is in the power of thine hand to do *it.*
Say not unto thy neighbour, Go, and come again, and to morrow I will give; when thou hast it by thee.
Devise not evil against thy neighbour, seeing he dwelleth securely by thee.
Strive not with a man without cause, if he have done thee no harm.

Proverbs 17:13:
Whoso rewardeth evil for good, evil shall not depart from his house.

Proverbs 25:21:
If thine enemy be hungry, give him bread to eat; and if he be thirsty, give him water to drink.

"Do not take fair weather friendships seriously."

Proverbs 17:17:
A friend loveth at all times, and a brother is born for adversity.

Proverbs 18:24:
A man *that hath* friends must shew himself friendly: and there is a friend *that* sticketh closer than a brother.

"Kindness affects more than severity."

Proverbs 12:10:
A righteous *man* regardeth the life of his beast: but the tender mercies of the wicked *are* cruel.

Proverbs 15:1:
A soft answer turneth away wrath: but grievous words stir up anger.

Proverbs 19:22:
The desire of a man *is* his kindness: and a poor man *is* better than a liar.

Proverbs 25:15:
By long forbearing is a prince persuaded, and a soft tongue breaketh the bone.

Proverbs 31:26:
She openeth her mouth with wisdom; and in her tongue *is* the law of kindness.

"Choose your friends well."

Proverbs 22:24:
Make no friendship with an angry man; and with a furious man thou shalt not go.

Proverbs 27:6,9,17:
Faithful *are* the wounds of a friend; but the kisses of an enemy *are* deceitful.
Ointment and perfume rejoice the heart: so *doth* the sweetness of a man's friend by hearty counsel.
Iron sharpeneth iron; so a man sharpeneth the countenance of his friend.

"People often grudge others what they cannot enjoy themselves."

Proverbs 3:27:
Withhold not good from them to whom it is due, when it is in the power of thine hand to do *it*.

Proverbs 11:24,26:
There is that scattereth, and yet increaseth; and *there is* that withholdeth more than is meet, but *it tendeth* to poverty.
He that withholdeth corn, the people shall curse him: but blessing *shall be* upon the head of him that selleth *it*.

"Zeal should not outrun discretion."

Proverbs 1:4:
To give subtilty to the simple, to the young man knowledge and discretion.

Proverbs 2:11:
Discretion shall preserve thee, understanding shall keep thee.

Proverbs 3:21:
My son, let not them depart from thine eyes: keep sound wisdom and discretion.

Proverbs 5:2:
That thou mayest regard discretion, and that thy lips may keep knowledge.

Proverbs 11:22:
As a jewel of gold in a swine's snout, so is a fair woman which is without discretion.

Proverbs 19:11:
The discretion of a man deferreth his anger; and it is his glory to pass over a transgression.

Proverbs 21:25:
The desire of the slothful killeth him; for his hands refuse to labour.

Proverbs 23:3,6:
Be not desirous of his dainties: for they *are* deceitful meat.
Eat thou not the bread of *him that hath* an evil eye, neither desire thou his dainty meats.

"Actions speak louder than words."

Proverbs 10:9:
He that walketh uprightly walketh surely: but he that perverteth his ways shall be known.

Proverbs 12:16:
A fool's wrath is presently known: but a prudent *man* covereth shame.

Proverbs 14:33:
Wisdom resteth in the heart of him that hath understanding: but *that which is* in the midst of fools is made known.

Proverbs 20:11:
Even a child is known by his doings, whether his work *be* pure, and whether *it be* right.

"One swallow does not make a summer."

Proverbs 29:20:
Seest thou a man *that is* hasty in his words? *there is* more hope of a fool than of him.

"Do not always take things for granted."

Proverbs 4:25:
Let thine eyes look right on, and let thine eyelids look straight before thee.

Proverbs 5:18:
Let thy fountain be blessed: and rejoice with the wife of thy youth.

Proverbs 27:23:
Be thou diligent to know the state of thy flocks, *and* look well to thy herds.

"Those who will not listen to flatterers will have a safer life."

Proverbs 2:16:
To deliver thee from the strange woman, *even* from the stranger *which* flattereth with her words.

Proverbs 6:24:
To keep thee from the evil woman, from the flattery of the tongue of a strange woman.

Proverbs 7:5,21:
That they may keep thee from the strange woman, from the stranger *which* flattereth with her words. With her much fair speech she caused him to yield, with the flattering of her lips she forced him.

Proverbs 20:19:
He that goeth about *as* a talebearer revealeth secrets: therefore meddle not with him that flattereth with his lips.

Proverbs 26:28:
A lying tongue hateth *those that are* afflicted by it; and a flattering mouth worketh ruin.

Proverbs 28:23:
He that rebuketh a man afterwards shall find more favour than he that flattereth with the tongue.

Proverbs 29:5:
A man that flattereth his neighbour spreadeth a net for his feet.

"A little thing in hand is worth more than a great thing in prospect."

Proverbs 5:15:
Drink waters out of thine own cistern, and running waters out of thine own well.

"It is easy to despise what you cannot get."

Proverbs 14:30:
A sound heart *is* the life of the flesh: but envy the rottenness of the bones.

Proverbs 23:17:
Let not thine heart envy sinners: but *be thou* in the fear of the Lord all the day long.

Proverbs 24:1,19:
Be not thou envious against evil men, neither desire to be with them.
Fret not thyself because of evil *men,* neither be thou envious at the wicked.

Proverbs 27:4:
Wrath *is* cruel, and anger *is* outrageous; but who *is* able to stand before envy?

"We can easily represent things as we wish them to be."

Proverbs 12:15:
The way of a fool *is* right in his own eyes: but he that hearkeneth unto counsel *is* wise.

Proverbs 16:2:
All the ways of a man *are* clean in his own eyes; but the Lord weigheth the spirits.

Proverbs 21:2:
Every way of a man *is* right in his own eyes: but the Lord pondereth the hearts.

Proverbs 30:12:
There is a generation *that are* pure in their own eyes, and *yet* is not washed from their filthiness.

"When one is well off it is not proper to complain."

Proverbs 16:20:
He that handleth a matter wisely shall find good: and whoso trusteth in the Lord, happy *is* he.

Proverbs 22:4:
By humility *and* the fear of the Lord *are* riches, and honour, and life.

"Character is often determined by your language."

Proverbs 6:2:
Thou art snared with the words of thy mouth, thou art taken with the words of thy mouth.

Proverbs 10:20,31
The tongue of the just *is as* choice silver: the heart of the wicked *is* little worth.
The mouth of the just bringeth forth wisdom: but the froward tongue shall be cut out.

Proverbs 12:18,19:
There is that speaketh like the piercings of a sword: but the tongue of the wise *is* health.
The lip of truth shall be established for ever: but a lying tongue *is* but for a moment.

Proverbs 15:2,4:
The tongue of the wise useth knowledge aright: but the mouth of fools poureth out foolishness.
A wholesome tongue *is* a tree of life: but perverseness therein *is* a breach in the spirit.

Proverbs 18:21:
Death and life *are* in the power of the tongue: and they that love it shall eat the fruit thereof.

"There is always someone worse off than yourself."

Proverbs 22:2:
The rich and poor meet together: the Lord *is* the maker of them all.

Proverbs 29:13:
The poor and the deceitful man meet together: the Lord lighteneth both their eyes.

"No gratitude from the wicked."

Proverbs 13:25:
The righteous eateth to the satisfying of his soul: but the belly of the wicked shall want.

Proverbs 15:28:
The heart of the righteous studieth to answer: but the mouth of the wicked poureth out evil things.

Proverbs 18:3:
When the wicked cometh, *then* cometh also contempt, and with ignominy reproach.

Proverbs 21:4,10, 29:
An high look, and a proud heart, *and* the plowing of the wicked, *is* sin.
The soul of the wicked desireth evil: his neighbour findeth no favour in his eyes.
A wicked man hardeneth his face: but *as for* the upright, he directeth his way.

"It is easy to be brave from a safe distance."

Proverbs 28:28:
When the wicked rise, men hide themselves: but when they perish, the righteous increase.

"Security is not gotten by treachery."

Proverbs 1:33:
But whoso hearkeneth unto me shall dwell safely, and shall be quiet from fear of evil.

Proverbs 11:14:
Where no counsel *is,* the people fall: but in the multitude of counsellors *there is* safety.

Proverbs 18:10:
The name of the Lord *is* a strong tower: the righteous runneth into it, and is safe.

Proverbs 19:5,9;
A false witness shall not be unpunished, and *he that* speaketh lies shall not escape.
A false witness shall not be unpunished, and *he that* speaketh lies shall perish.

Proverbs 21:28,31:
A false witness shall perish: but the man that heareth speaketh constantly.
The horse *is* prepared against the day of battle: but safety *is* of the Lord.

Proverbs 24:6
For by wise counsel thou shalt make thy war: and in multitude of counsellors *there is* safety.

Proverbs 29:25
The fear of man bringeth a snare: but whoso putteth his trust in the Lord shall be safe.

"Familiarity breeds contempt."

Proverbs 18:3,19,24:
When the wicked cometh, *then* cometh also contempt, and with ignominy reproach.
A brother offended *is harder to be won* than a strong city: and *their* contentions *are* like the bars of a castle.
A man *that hath* friends must shew himself friendly: and there is a friend *that* sticketh closer than a brother.

"It's impossible to bribe a natural servant."

Proverbs 14:35:
The king's favour *is* toward a wise servant: but his wrath is *against* him that causeth shame.

Proverbs 15:27:
He that is greedy of gain troubleth his own house; but he that hateth gifts shall live.

Proverbs 17:2:
A wise servant shall have rule over a son that causeth shame, and shall have part of the inheritance among the brethren.

Proverbs 28:21:
To have respect of persons *is* not good: for for a piece of bread *that* man will transgress.

"Better no rule than cruel rule."

Proverbs 28:15:
As a roaring lion, and a ranging bear; *so is* a wicked ruler over the poor people.

Proverbs 29:2:
When the righteous are in authority, the people rejoice: but when the wicked beareth rule, the people mourn.

"Do not be proud of being a fool."

Proverbs 14:3:
In the mouth of the foolish *is* a rod of pride: but the lips of the wise shall preserve them.

"True pity is not to be judged by tears."

Proverbs 23:7:
For as he thinketh in his heart, so *is* he: Eat and drink, saith he to thee; but his heart *is* not with thee.

Proverbs 27:6:
Faithful *are* the wounds of a friend; but the kisses of an enemy *are* deceitful.

"Wealth unused might as well not exist."

Proverbs 11:4:
Riches profit not in the day of wrath: but righteousness delivereth from death.

Proverbs 13:7,11:
There is that maketh himself rich, yet *hath* nothing: *there is* that maketh himself poor, yet *hath* great riches.
Wealth *gotten* by vanity shall be diminished: but he that gathereth by labour shall increase.

"No help should be given to the wicked."

Proverbs 4:14:
Enter not into the path of the wicked, and go not in the way of evil *men*.

Proverbs 14:16:
A wise *man* feareth, and departeth from evil: but the fool rageth, and is confident.

Proverbs 17:15:
He that justifieth the wicked, and he that condemneth the just, even they both *are* abomination to the Lord.

Proverbs 18:5:
The heart of the prudent getteth knowledge; and the ear of the wise seeketh knowledge.

Proverbs 22:3:
A prudent *man* foreseeth the evil, and hideth himself: but the simple pass on, and are punished.

Proverbs 23:6:
Eat thou not the bread of *him that hath* an evil eye, neither desire thou his dainty meats.

Proverbs 24:24:
He that saith unto the wicked, Thou *art* righteous; him shall the people curse, nations shall abhor him.

Proverbs 28:4:
They that forsake the law praise the wicked: but such as keep the law contend with them.

"Manners always speak louder than words."

Proverbs 10:9:
In the multitude of words there wanteth not sin: but he that refraineth his lips *is* wise.

Proverbs 12:16:
A fool's wrath is presently known: but a prudent *man* covereth shame.

Proverbs 14:33:
Wisdom resteth in the heart of him that hath understanding: but *that which is* in the midst of fools is made known.

Proverbs 20:11:
Even a child is known by his doings, whether his work *be* pure, and whether *it be* right.

"Only the ill-bred mock at others."

Proverbs 14:9:
Fools make a mock at sin: but among the righteous *there is* favour.

Proverbs 17:5:
Whoso mocketh the poor reproacheth his Maker: *and* he that is glad at calamities shall not be unpunished.

Proverbs 30:17:
The eye *that* mocketh at *his* father, and despiseth to obey *his* mother, the ravens of the valley shall pick it out, and the young eagles shall eat it.

"Be content with your lot; one cannot be first in everything."

Proverbs 14:30:
A sound heart *is* the life of the flesh: but envy the rottenness of the bones.

Proverbs 16:19:
Better *it is to be* of an humble spirit with the lowly, than to divide the spoil with the proud.

Proverbs 18:17:
He that is first in his own cause *seemeth* just; but his neighbour cometh and searcheth him.

Proverbs 23:17:
Let not thine heart envy sinners: but *be thou* in the fear of the Lord all the day long.

Proverbs 27:4:
Wrath *is* cruel, and anger *is* outrageous; but who *is* able to stand before envy?

"Never trust the advice of a man in difficulties."

Proverbs 12:5:
The thoughts of the righteous *are* right: *but* the counsels of the wicked *are* deceit.

"To only imitate does not create great character."

Proverbs 20:23:
Divers weights *are* an abomination unto the Lord; and a false balance *is* not good.

Proverbs 25:14:
Whoso boasteth himself of a false gift *is like* clouds and wind without rain.

"The easy way is not always the best."

Proverbs 14:29:
He that is slow to wrath *is* of great understanding: but *he that is* hasty of spirit exalteth folly.

Proverbs 19:2:
Also, *that* the soul *be* without knowledge, *it is* not good; and he that hasteth with *his* feet sinneth.

Proverbs 21:5:
The thoughts of the diligent *tend* only to plenteousness; but of every one *that is* hasty only to want.

Proverbs 28:20,22:
A faithful man shall abound with blessings: but he that maketh haste to be rich shall not be innocent. He that hasteth to be rich *hath* an evil eye, and considereth not that poverty shall come upon him.

"Nothing escapes the master's eye."

Proverbs 8:20:
I lead in the way of righteousness, in the midst of the paths of judgment.

Proverbs 10:14:
Wise *men* lay up knowledge: but the mouth of the foolish *is* near destruction.

Proverbs 15:3:
The eyes of the Lord *are* in every place, beholding the evil and the good.
Proverbs 20:8:
A king that sitteth in the throne of judgment scattereth away all evil with his eyes.

Proverbs 24:5,18:
A wise man *is* strong; yea, a man of knowledge increaseth strength.
Lest the Lord see *it,* and it displease him, and he turn away his wrath from him.

"Humble occupation is often a security."

Proverbs 3:34:
Surely he scorneth the scorners: but he giveth grace unto the lowly.

Proverbs 11:2:
When pride cometh, then cometh shame: but with the lowly *is* wisdom.

Proverbs 16:19:
Better *it is to be* of an humble spirit with the lowly, than to divide the spoil with the proud.

"Be not too easily led."

Proverbs 1:15:
My son, walk not thou in the way with them; refrain thy foot from their path.

Proverbs 2:12:
To deliver thee from the way of the evil *man,* from the man that speaketh froward things.

Proverbs 4:1:
Hear, ye children, the instruction of a father, and attend to know understanding.

Proverbs 6:24:
To keep thee from the evil woman, from the flattery of the tongue of a strange woman.

Proverbs 7:5:
That they may keep thee from the strange woman, from the stranger *which* flattereth with her words.

Proverbs 12:11:
He that tilleth his land shall be satisfied with bread: but he that followeth vain *persons is* void of understanding.

"Falsehood leads to destruction."

Proverbs 19:5,9:
A false witness shall not be unpunished, and *he that* speaketh lies shall not escape.
A false witness shall not be unpunished, and *he that* speaketh lies shall perish.

Proverbs 21:8:
The way of man *is* froward and strange: but *as for* the pure, his work *is* right.

Proverbs 25:18:
A man that beareth false witness against his neighbour *is* a maul, and a sword, and a sharp arrow.

"Home is always safer than strange places."

Proverbs 5:15-20:
Drink waters out of thine own cistern, and running waters out of thine own well.
Let thy fountains be dispersed abroad, *and* rivers of waters in the streets.
Let them be only thine own, and not strangers' with thee.
Let thy fountain be blessed: and rejoice with the wife of thy youth.
Let her be as the loving hind and pleasant roe; let her breasts satisfy thee at all times; and be thou ravished always with her love.
And why wilt thou, my son, be ravished with a strange woman, and embrace the bosom of a stranger?

Proverbs 27:8:
As a bird that wandereth from her nest, so *is* a man that wandereth from his place.

"Self-conceit may lead to self-destruction."

Proverbs 5:22:
His own iniquities shall take the wicked himself, and he shall be holden with the cords of his sins.

Proverbs 12:9:
He that is despised, and hath a servant, *is* better than he that honoureth himself, and lacketh bread.

Proverbs 18:2:
A fool hath no delight in understanding, but that his heart may discover itself.

Proverbs 25:6,14:
Put not forth thyself in the presence of the king, and stand not in the place of great *men*.
Whoso boasteth himself of a false gift *is like* clouds and wind without rain.

Proverbs 27:1:
Boast not thyself of to morrow; for thou knowest not what a day may bring forth.

"We can never be too carefully guarded against acquaintance with persons of bad character."

Proverbs 1:8,10,14,15:
My son, hear the instruction of thy father, and forsake not the law of thy mother.
My son, if sinners entice thee, consent thou not.
Cast in thy lot among us; let us all have one purse:
My son, walk not thou in the way with them; refrain thy foot from their path.

Proverbs 4:14-16:
Enter not into the path of the wicked, and go not in the way of evil *men*.
Avoid it, pass not by it, turn from it, and pass away.
For they sleep not, except they have done mischief; and their sleep is taken away, unless they cause *some* to fall.

Proverbs 7:25:
Let not thine heart decline to her ways, go not astray in her paths.

Proverbs 21:12:
The righteous *man* wisely considereth the house of the wicked: *but God* overthroweth the wicked for *their* wickedness.

Proverbs 14:15:
The simple believeth every word: but the prudent man looketh well to his going.

Proverbs 22:3:
A prudent man foreseeth the evil, and hideth himself: but the simple pass on, and are punished.

Proverbs 25:8,26:
Go not forth hastily to strive, lest *thou know not* what to do in the end thereof, when thy neighbour hath put thee to shame.
A righteous man falling down before the wicked *is as* a troubled fountain, and a corrupt spring.

Proverbs 27:12:
A prudent man foreseeth the evil, and hideth himself; but the simple pass on, and are punished.

"It is useless attacking the insensible."

Proverbs 9:7,8:
He that reproveth a scorner getteth to himself shame: and he that rebuketh a wicked *man getteth* himself a blot.
Reprove not a scorner, lest he hate thee: rebuke a wise man, and he will love thee.

Proverbs 10:17:
He *is in* the way of life that keepeth instruction: but he that refuseth reproof erreth.

Proverbs 12:1:
Whoso loveth instruction loveth knowledge: but he that hateth reproof *is* brutish.

Proverbs 17:10:
A reproof entereth more into a wise man than an hundred stripes into a fool.

Proverbs 21:29:
It is better to dwell in a corner of the housetop, than with a brawling woman in a wide house.

Proverbs 28:14:
Happy *is* the man that feareth alway: but he that hardeneth his heart shall fall into mischief.

Proverbs 29:1:
He, that being often reproved hardeneth *his* neck, shall suddenly be destroyed, and that without remedy.

"Love can tame the wildest."

Proverbs 14:29:
He that is slow to wrath *is* of great understanding: but *he that is* hasty of spirit exalteth folly.

Proverbs 15:1,18:
A soft answer turneth away wrath: but grievous words stir up anger.
A wrathful man stirreth up strife: but *he that is* slow to anger appeaseth strife.

Proverbs 16:32:
He that is slow to anger *is* better than the mighty; and he that ruleth his spirit than he that taketh a city.

Proverbs 25:15:
By long forbearing is a prince persuaded, and a soft tongue breaketh the bone.

"Do not follow bad advice."

Proverbs 12:5:
The thoughts of the righteous *are* right: *but* the counsels of the wicked *are* deceit.

Proverbs 13:10:
Only by pride cometh contention: but with the well advised *is* wisdom.

Proverbs 20:18:
Every purpose is established by counsel: and with good advice make war.

"Every tale is not to be believed."

Proverbs 17:4:
A wicked doer giveth heed to false lips; *and* a liar giveth ear to a naughty tongue.

Proverbs 14:15:
The simple believeth every word: but the prudent *man* looketh well to his going.

Proverbs 26:25:
When he speaketh fair, believe him not: for *there are* seven abominations in his heart.

"Beware lest you lose the substance by grasping at the shadow."

Proverbs 2:13:
Who leave the paths of uprightness, to walk in the ways of darkness.

Proverbs 4:19:
The way of the wicked *is* as darkness: they know not at what they stumble.

"It is unwise to neglect a useful tool, even when not in use."

Proverbs 12:10, 27:
A righteous *man* regardeth the life of his beast: but the tender mercies of the wicked *are* cruel.
The slothful *man* roasteth not that which he took in hunting: but the substance of a diligent man *is* precious.

Proverbs 18:9:
He also that is slothful in his work is brother to him that is a great waster.

Proverbs 19:26:
He that wasteth *his* father, *and* chaseth away *his* mother, *is* a son that causeth shame, and bringeth reproach.

"Men often applaud an imitation, and hiss the real thing."

Proverbs 1:7:
The fear of the Lord *is* the beginning of knowledge: *but* fools despise wisdom and instruction.

Proverbs 15:5,20:
A fool despiseth his father's instruction: but he that regardeth reproof is prudent.
A wise son maketh a glad father: but a foolish man despiseth his mother.

"Hard blows will not keep a good man down."

Proverbs 24:16:
For a just *man* falleth seven times, and riseth up again: but the wicked shall fall into mischief.

Proverbs 28:18:
Whoso walketh uprightly shall be saved: but *he that is* perverse *in his* ways shall fall at once.

"You cannot escape your fate."

Proverbs 21:30:
There is no wisdom nor understanding nor counsel against the Lord.

"What is worth most is often valued least."

Proverbs 1:7:
The fear of the Lord *is* the beginning of knowledge: *but* fools despise wisdom and instruction.

Proverbs 1:30:
They would none of my counsel: they despised all my reproof.

Proverbs 3:11:
My son, despise not the chastening of the Lord; neither be weary of his correction.

Proverbs 5:12:
And say, How have I hated instruction, and my heart despised reproof.

Proverbs 13:13:
Whoso despiseth the word shall be destroyed: but he that feareth the commandment shall be rewarded.

Proverbs 14:2:
He that walketh in his uprightness feareth the Lord: but *he that is* perverse in his ways despiseth him.

Proverbs 15:5:
A fool despiseth his father's instruction: but he that regardeth reproof is prudent.

Proverbs 15:20,32:
A wise son maketh a glad father: but a foolish man despiseth his mother.
He that refuseth instruction despiseth his own soul: but he that heareth reproof getteth understanding.

Proverbs 19:16:
He that keepeth the commandment keepeth his own soul; *but* he that despiseth his ways shall die.

Proverbs 23:9,22:
Speak not in the ears of a fool: for he will despise the wisdom of thy words.
Hearken unto thy father that begat thee, and despise not thy mother when she is old.

Proverbs 30:17:
The eye *that* mocketh at *his* father, and despiseth to obey *his* mother, the ravens of the valley shall pick it out, and the young eagles shall eat it.

"Rewards are never gained by treachery."

Proverbs 11:18:
The wicked worketh a deceitful work: but to him that soweth righteousness *shall be* a sure reward.

Proverbs 17:13:
Whoso rewardeth evil for good, evil shall not depart from his house.

Proverbs 24:20:
For there shall be no reward to the evil *man;* the candle of the wicked shall be put out.

Proverbs 25:22:
For thou shalt heap coals of fire upon his head, and the Lord shall reward thee.

"Appearances are deceptive."

Proverbs 11:18:
The wicked worketh a deceitful work: but to him that soweth righteousness *shall be* a sure reward.

Proverbs 12:5,17,20:
The thoughts of the righteous *are* right: *but* the counsels of the wicked *are* deceit.
He that speaketh truth sheweth forth righteousness: but a false witness deceit.
Deceit *is* in the heart of them that imagine evil: but to the counsellors of peace *is* joy.

Proverbs 14:8,25:
The wisdom of the prudent *is* to understand his way: but the folly of fools *is* deceit.
A true witness delivereth souls: but a deceitful *witness* speaketh lies.

Proverbs 20:17:
Bread of deceit *is* sweet to a man; but afterwards his mouth shall be filled with gravel.

Proverbs 23:3,7:
Be not desirous of his dainties: for they *are* deceitful meat.
For as he thinketh in his heart, so *is* he: Eat and drink, saith he to thee; but his heart *is* not with thee.

Proverbs 26:19,24:
So *is* the man *that* deceiveth his neighbour, and saith, Am not I in sport?
He that hateth dissembleth with his lips, and layeth up deceit within him.

Proverbs 26:26:
Whose hatred is covered by deceit, his wickedness shall be shewed before the *whole* congregation.

Proverbs 27:6:
Faithful *are* the wounds of a friend; but the kisses of an enemy *are* deceitful.

"Destroy the seed of evil, or it will grow up to your ruin."

Proverbs 2:17:
Which forsaketh the guide of her youth, and forgetteth the covenant of her God.

Proverbs 7:7:
And beheld among the simple ones, I discerned among the youths, a young man void of understanding.

Proverbs 22:8:
He that soweth iniquity shall reap vanity: and the rod of his anger shall fail.

"Any excuse will serve a tyrant."

Proverbs 16:12:
It is an abomination to kings to commit wickedness: for the throne is established by righteousness.

Proverbs 18:23:
The poor useth intreaties; but the rich answereth roughly.

Proverbs 25:5:
Take away the wicked *from* before the king, and his throne shall be established in righteousness.

Proverbs 28:15:
As a roaring lion, and a ranging bear; *so is* a wicked ruler over the poor people.

Proverbs 29:2:
When the righteous are in authority, the people rejoice: but when the wicked beareth rule, the people mourn.

"Do not count your chickens before they are hatched."

Proverbs 18:13:
He that answereth a matter before he heareth *it*, it *is* folly and shame unto him.

Proverbs 20:22:
Say not thou, I will recompense evil; *but* wait on the Lord, and he shall save thee.

Proverbs 27:1:
Boast not thyself of to morrow; for thou knowest not what a day may bring forth.

"Fine clothes may disguise, but silly words will disclose a fool."

Proverbs 10:14:
Wise *men* lay up knowledge: but the mouth of the foolish *is* near destruction.

Proverbs 11:22:
As a jewel of gold in a swine's snout, *so is* a fair woman which is without discretion.

Proverbs 14:3,7:
In the mouth of the foolish *is* a rod of pride: but the lips of the wise shall preserve them.
Go from the presence of a foolish man, when thou perceivest not *in him* the lips of knowledge.

Proverbs 15:2,14:
The tongue of the wise useth knowledge aright: but the mouth of fools poureth out foolishness.
The heart of him that hath understanding seeketh knowledge: but the mouth of fools feedeth on foolishness.

Proverbs 17:28:
Even a fool, when he holdeth his peace, is counted wise: *and* he that shutteth his lips *is esteemed* a man of understanding.

Proverbs 18:6,7:
A fool's lips enter into contention, and his mouth calleth for strokes.
A fool's mouth *is* his destruction, and his lips *are* the snare of his soul.

Proverbs 26:7,9:
The legs of the lame are not equal: so *is* a parable in the mouth of fools.
As a thorn goeth up into the hand of a drunkard, so *is* a parable in the mouth of fools.

"Enemies' promises were made to be broken."

Proverbs 27:6:
Faithful *are* the wounds of a friend; but the kisses of an enemy *are* deceitful.

"He that is neither one thing nor the other has no friends."

Proverbs 14:20:
The poor is hated even of his own neighbour: but the rich *hath* many friends.

Proverbs 19:7:
All the brethren of the poor do hate him: how much more do his friends go far from him? he pursueth *them with* words, *yet* they *are* wanting *to him.*

"Never accept interested advice."

Proverbs 12:5:
The thoughts of the righteous *are* right: *but* the counsels of the wicked *are* deceit.

Proverbs 13:10:
Only by pride cometh contention: but with the well advised *is* wisdom.

Proverbs 20:18:
Every purpose is established by counsel: and with good advice make war.

"Do not try to take credit that is due to others."

Proverbs 9:12:
If thou be wise, thou shalt be wise for thyself: but *if* thou scornest, thou alone shalt bear *it.*

Proverbs 12:9:
He that is despised, and hath a servant, *is* better than he that honoureth himself, and lacketh bread.

Proverbs 20:6:
Most men will proclaim every one his own goodness: but a faithful man who can find?

Proverbs 25:6,14:
Put not forth thyself in the presence of the king, and stand not in the place of great *men.*
Whoso boasteth himself of a false gift *is like* clouds and wind without rain.

Proverbs 27:1:
Boast not thyself of to morrow; for thou knowest not what a day may bring forth.

Proverbs 30:32:
If thou hast done foolishly in lifting up thyself, or if thou hast thought evil, *lay* thine hand upon thy mouth.

"Pleasure brought with pains, hurts."

Proverbs 14:10,13:
The heart knoweth his own bitterness; and a stranger doth not intermeddle with his joy.
Even in laughter the heart is sorrowful; and the end of that mirth *is* heaviness.

"Practice what you preach."

Proverbs 4:4:
He taught me also, and said unto me, Let thine heart retain my words: keep my commandments, and live.

Proverbs 6:2:
Thou art snared with the words of thy mouth, thou art taken with the words of thy mouth.

Proverbs 7:2:
Keep my commandments, and live; and my law as the apple of thine eye.

Proverbs 9:6:
Forsake the foolish, and live; and go in the way of understanding.

"You a king, and not understand a trap!"

Proverbs 16:12:
It is an abomination to kings to commit wickedness: for the throne is established by righteousness.

Proverbs 25:5:
Take away the wicked *from* before the king, and his throne shall be established in righteousness.

Proverbs 29:4:
The king by judgment establisheth the land: but he that receiveth gifts overthroweth it.

Proverbs 31:3,4:
Give not thy strength unto women, nor thy ways to that which destroyeth kings.
It is not for kings, O Lemuel, *it is* not for kings to drink wine; nor for princes strong drink.

"A heavy load is a sure cure for conceit."

Proverbs 11:2:
When pride cometh, then cometh shame: but with the lowly *is* wisdom.

Proverbs 13:10:
Only by pride cometh contention: but with the well advised *is* wisdom.

Proverbs 16:18:
Pride *goeth* before destruction, and an haughty spirit before a fall.

Proverbs 26:5:
Answer a fool according to his folly, lest he be wise in his own conceit.

Proverbs 29:23:
A man's pride shall bring him low: but honour shall uphold the humble in spirit.

"Better humble security than gilded danger."

Proverbs 3:14:
For the merchandise of it *is* better than the merchandise of silver, and the gain thereof than fine gold.

Proverbs 8:11,19:
For wisdom *is* better than rubies; and all the things that may be desired are not to be compared to it.
My fruit *is* better than gold, yea, than fine gold; and my revenue than choice silver.

Proverbs 12:9:
He that is despised, and hath a servant, *is* better than he that honoureth himself, and lacketh bread.

Proverbs 15:16,17:
Better *is* little with the fear of the Lord than great treasure and trouble therewith.
Better *is* a dinner of herbs where love is, than a stalled ox and hatred therewith.

Proverbs 16:8,16,19,32:
Better *is* a little with righteousness than great revenues without right.
How much better *is it* to get wisdom than gold! and to get understanding rather to be chosen than silver!
Better *it is to be* of an humble spirit with the lowly, than to divide the spoil with the proud.
He that is slow to anger *is* better than the mighty; and he that ruleth his spirit than he that taketh a city.

Proverbs 17:1:
Better *is* a dry morsel, and quietness therewith, than an house full of sacrifices *with* strife.

Proverbs 19:1,22:
Better *is* the poor that walketh in his integrity, than *he that is* perverse in his lips, and is a fool.
The desire of a man *is* his kindness: and a poor man *is* better than a liar.

Proverbs 21:9,19:
It is better to dwell in a corner of the housetop, than with a brawling woman in a wide house.
It is better to dwell in the wilderness, than with a contentious and an angry woman.

Proverbs 25:7:
For better *it is* that it be said unto thee, Come up hither; than that thou shouldest be put lower in the presence of the prince whom thine eyes have seen.

Proverbs 27:5,10:
Open rebuke *is* better than secret love.
Thine own friend, and thy father's friend, forsake not; neither go into thy brother's house in the day of thy calamity: *for* better *is* a neighbour *that is* near than a brother far off.

"Obscurity often brings safety."

Proverbs 18:10:
The name of the Lord *is* a strong tower: the righteous runneth into it, and is safe.

Proverbs 21:31:
The horse *is* prepared against the day of battle: but safety *is* of the Lord.

Proverbs 29:25:
The fear of man bringeth a snare: but whoso putteth his trust in the Lord shall be safe.

"As ye sow, so shall ye reap."

Proverbs 1:31:
Therefore shall they eat of the fruit of their own way, and be filled with their own devices.

Proverbs 11:31:
Behold, the righteous shall be recompensed in the earth: much more the wicked and the sinner.

Proverbs 26:27:
Whoso diggeth a pit shall fall therein: and he that rolleth a stone, it will return upon him.

"Interested advisers usually are seeking some gift."

Proverbs 12:5:
The thoughts of the righteous *are* right: *but* the counsels of the wicked *are* deceit.

Proverbs 13:10:
Only by pride cometh contention: but with the well advised *is* wisdom.

Proverbs 20:18:
Every purpose is established by counsel: and with good advice make war.

"Self-importance means little to the truly wise."

Proverbs 14:3:
In the mouth of the foolish *is* a rod of pride: but the lips of the wise shall preserve them.

Proverbs 16:18:
Pride *goeth* before destruction, and an haughty spirit before a fall.

Proverbs 18:12:
Before destruction the heart of man is haughty, and before honour *is* humility.

"To be unhappy, complain about your lot."

Proverbs 12:11,14:
He that tilleth his land shall be satisfied with bread: but he that followeth vain *persons is* void of understanding.
A man shall be satisfied with good by the fruit of *his mouth:* and the recompence of a man's hands shall be rendered unto him.

Proverbs 13:25:
The righteous eateth to the satisfying of his soul: but the belly of the wicked shall want.

Proverbs 14:14:
The backslider in heart shall be filled with his own ways: and a good man *shall be satisfied* from himself.

Proverbs 18:20:
A man's belly shall be satisfied with the fruit of his mouth; *and* with the increase of his lips shall he be filled.

Proverbs 19:23:
The fear of the Lord *tendeth* to life: and *he that hath it* shall abide satisfied; he shall not be visited with evil.

Proverbs 20:13:
Love not sleep, lest thou come to poverty; open thine eyes, *and* thou shalt be satisfied with bread.

"Better starve free, than be a fat slave."

Proverbs 11:17:
The merciful man doeth good to his own soul: but *he that is* cruel troubleth his own flesh.

Proverbs 16:19:
Better *it is to be* of an humble spirit with the lowly, than to divide the spoil with the proud.

Proverbs 17:2:
A wise servant shall have rule over a son that causeth shame, and shall have part of the inheritance among the brethren.

Proverbs 28:6:
Better *is* the poor that walketh in his uprightness, than *he that is* perverse *in his* ways, though he *be* rich.

"A cobbler should stick to his last."

Proverbs 12:9:
He that is despised, and hath a servant, *is* better than he that honoureth himself, and lacketh bread.

Proverbs 19:10:
Delight is not seemly for a fool; much less for a servant to have rule over princes.

Proverbs 23:4:
Labour not to be rich: cease from thine own wisdom.

Proverbs 25:6:
Put not forth thyself in the presence of the king, and stand not in the place of great *men*.

"Flattery is not a proof of true admiration."

Proverbs 2:16:
To deliver thee from the strange woman, even from the stranger which flattereth with her words.

Proverbs 6:24:
To keep thee from the evil woman, from the flattery of the tongue of a strange woman.

Proverbs 7:5,21:
That they may keep thee from the strange woman, from the stranger which flattereth with her words.
With her much fair speech she caused him to yield, with the flattering of her lips she forced him.

Proverbs 20:19:
He that goeth about as a talebearer revealeth secrets: therefore meddle not with him that flattereth with his lips.

Proverbs 23:7:
For as he thinketh in his heart, so *is* he: Eat and drink, saith he to thee; but his heart *is* not with thee.

Proverbs 26:28:
A lying tongue hateth those that are afflicted by it; and a flattering mouth worketh ruin.

"Fine-weather friends are not worth much."

Proverbs 3:27,28:
Withhold not good from them to whom it is due, when it is in the power of thine hand to do *it*.
Say not unto thy neighbour, Go, and come again, and to morrow I will give; when thou hast it by thee.

Proverbs 22:4:
By humility *and* the fear of the Lord *are* riches, and honour, and life.

"Better beans and bacon in peace, than cakes and ale in fear."

Proverbs 11:17:
The merciful man doeth good to his own soul: but *he that is* cruel troubleth his own flesh.

Proverbs 15:15,16:
All the days of the afflicted *are* evil: but he that is of a merry heart *hath* a continual feast.
Better *is* little with the fear of the Lord than great treasure and trouble therewith.

Proverbs 16:19:
Better *it is to be* of an humble spirit with the lowly, than to divide the spoil with the proud.

Proverbs 17:1:
Better *is* a dry morsel, and quietness therewith, than an house full of sacrifices *with* strife.

"It is easier to get into the enemy's toils than out again."

Proverbs 4:16:
For they sleep not, except they have done mischief; and their sleep is taken away, unless they cause *some* to fall.

Proverbs 6:1,2:
My son, if thou be surety for thy friend, *if* thou hast stricken thy hand with a stranger,
Thou art snared with the words of thy mouth, thou art taken with the words of thy mouth.

Proverbs 11:12:
He that is void of wisdom despiseth his neighbour: but a man of understanding holdeth his peace.

Proverbs 16:5:
Every one *that is* proud in heart *is* an abomination to the Lord: *though* hand *join* in hand, he shall not be unpunished.

Proverbs 17:18:
A man void of understanding striketh hands, *and* becometh surety in the presence of his friend.

Proverbs 22:26:
Be not thou *one* of them that strike hands, *or* of them that are sureties for debts.

"We had better bear our troubles bravely than try to escape them."

Proverbs 9:12:
If thou be wise, thou shalt be wise for thyself: but *if* thou scornest, thou alone shalt bear *it.*

Proverbs 28:1:
The wicked flee when no man pursueth: but the righteous are bold as a lion.

"It is easy to propose impossible remedies."

Proverbs 4:24:
Put away from thee a froward mouth, and perverse lips put far from thee.

Proverbs 6:12:
A naughty person, a wicked man, walketh with a froward mouth.

Proverbs 10:31,32:
The mouth of the just bringeth forth wisdom: but the froward tongue shall be cut out.
The lips of the righteous know what is acceptable: but the mouth of the wicked *speaketh* frowardness.

Proverbs 12:20:
Deceit *is* in the heart of them that imagine evil: but to the counsellors of peace *is* joy.

"Your enemies will use any excuse to attack you."

Proverbs 16:12:
It is an abomination to kings to commit wickedness: for the throne is established by righteousness.

Proverbs 18:23:
The poor useth intreaties; but the rich answereth roughly.

Proverbs 25:5:
Take away the wicked *from* before the king, and his throne shall be established in righteousness.

Proverbs 28:15:
As a roaring lion, and a ranging bear; *so is* a wicked ruler over the poor people.

Proverbs 29:2:
When the righteous are in authority, the people rejoice: but when the wicked beareth rule, the people mourn.

"Sure, those who have neither strength nor weapons to fight at least should be civil."

Proverbs 3:27:
Withhold not good from them to whom it is due, when it is in the power of thine hand to do *it*.

Proverbs 18:23:
The poor useth intreaties; but the rich answereth roughly.

"Use your given powers with judgment."

Proverbs 1:3:
To receive the instruction of wisdom, justice, and judgment, and equity.

Proverbs 18:16:
A man's gift maketh room for him, and bringeth him before great men.

Proverbs 21:3:
To do justice and judgment *is* more acceptable to the Lord than sacrifice.

"You may share the labors of the great, but you will not share the spoil."

Proverbs 3:27:
Withhold not good from them to whom it is due, when it is in the power of thine hand to do *it*.

Proverbs 11:24:
There is that scattereth, and yet increaseth; and *there is* that withholdeth more than is meet, but *it tendeth* to poverty.

Proverbs 18:23:
The poor useth intreaties; but the rich answereth roughly.

Proverbs 28:11,15:
The rich man *is* wise in his own conceit; but the poor that hath understanding searcheth him out.
As a roaring lion, and a ranging bear; *so is* a wicked ruler over the poor people.

"Everyone should know his Master."

Proverbs 25:13:
As the cold of snow in the time of harvest, *so is* a faithful messenger to them that send him: for he refresheth the soul of his masters.

Proverbs 27:18:
Whoso keepeth the fig tree shall eat the fruit thereof: so he that waiteth on his master shall be honoured.

"The man who talks for both sides is not to be trusted."

Proverbs 11:7,13:
When a wicked man dieth, *his* expectation shall perish: and the hope of unjust *men* perisheth.
A talebearer revealeth secrets: but he that is of a faithful spirit concealeth the matter.

Proverbs 18:8:
The words of a talebearer *are* as wounds, and they go down into the innermost parts of the belly.

Proverbs 20:19:
He that goeth about *as* a talebearer revealeth secrets: therefore meddle not with him that flattereth with his lips.

Proverbs 26:20,22:
Where no wood is, *there* the fire goeth out: so where *there is* no talebearer, the strife ceaseth.
The words of a talebearer *are* as wounds, and they go down into the innermost parts of the belly.

"Do not let your vanity make you overestimate your powers."

Proverbs 8:13:
The fear of the Lord *is* to hate evil: pride, and arrogancy, and the evil way, and the froward mouth, do I hate.

Proverbs 11:2:
When pride cometh, then cometh shame: but with the lowly *is* wisdom.

Proverbs 13:10:
Only by pride cometh contention: but with the well advised *is* wisdom.

Proverbs 14:3:
In the mouth of the foolish *is* a rod of pride: but the lips of the wise shall preserve them.

Proverbs 16:18:
Pride *goeth* before destruction, and an haughty spirit before a fall.

"A liar will not be believed, even when he speaks the truth."

Proverbs 26:25:
When he speaketh fair, believe him not: for *there are* seven abominations in his heart.

"Gratitude and greed go not together."

Proverbs 1:19:
So *are* the ways of every one that is greedy of gain; *which* taketh away the life of the owners thereof.

Proverbs 15:27:
He that is greedy of gain troubleth his own house; but he that hateth gifts shall live.

"The least of our enemies is the most to be feared."

Proverbs 27:6:
Faithful *are* the wounds of a friend; but the kisses of an enemy *are* deceitful.

About the Author

Eugene M. Slavit was born in St. Louis, Missouri in 1955. Since 1975, Gene has devoted his life to serving the Lord Jesus Christ and teaching the scriptures that declare him. During his time at the University of Missouri, he discovered the great riches in both the Old and New Testaments. As a graduate of the university's Classical Studies Department, he had access to renowned Greek and Latin teachers, including Meyer Reinhold. He translated from Latin and Greek, as with Aesop's Fables and other writing. Since that time, he has served as adjunct Greek faculty for three Bible colleges and continues to post his studies on the website freedomlifelight.com with his wife's able support.

Gene began cartooning with his best friend, Steve, in grade school. They invented their own characters and made simple comic strips. In high school, Gene's friend William taught him about comic-book art and how to draw in a simple and illuminating style. Gene took art classes at the University of Missouri with a focus on anatomical drawing.

Gene met Sherry while studying at a Bible college. Married for almost forty years, they've had many adventures in Australia, New Zealand, Guam, the Philippines, Korea, Okinawa, Japan, Israel, and Ireland. Sherry's Dad gave them a copy of Aesop's Fables, which Gene had read in elementary school along with Greek myths and stories.

Elijah, Gene and Sherry's only child, lives with his loving wife Aimee and their daughter Florence Aeterna. He serves in the United States Air Force, and is a Bible student and teacher.

Gene and Sherry live in Rancho Palos Verdes, California. Gene enjoys walks with Sherry, visiting family, writing, drawing, running, hiking, swimming in the ocean, teaching at a local classical academy, and sharing God's Word with old and new friends.

Other Books for Children by Gene Slavit

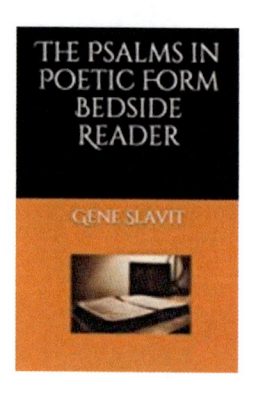

All 150 Psalms are precisely translated into rhyming English poetry from the original Hebrew Biblical text. Comforting reading for children at bedtime.

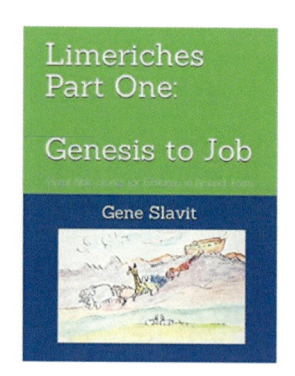

120 fables adapted to Biblical stories, with watercolor illustrations for each revisited fable. A special appendix gives morals in relation to Solomon's Proverbs.

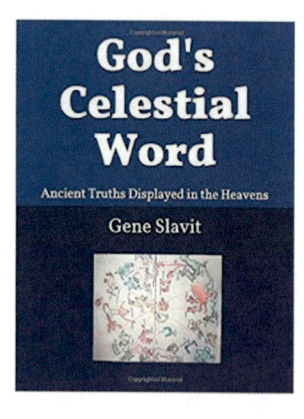

This book gives groundbreaking new insights into the purpose of the stars and the great story that they tell. Complete with 50 original full-color watercolor illustrations.

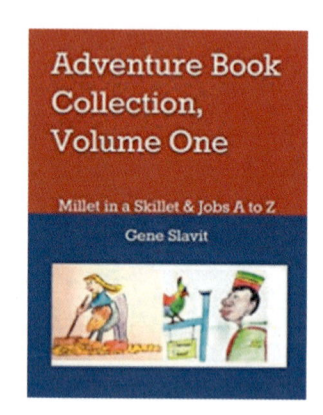

JOBS A to Z teaches children about occupations in rhyming alliterative poetry. Millet in the Skillet builds phonic skills. Plus Have You Ever Seen a Butterfly Flutter by?

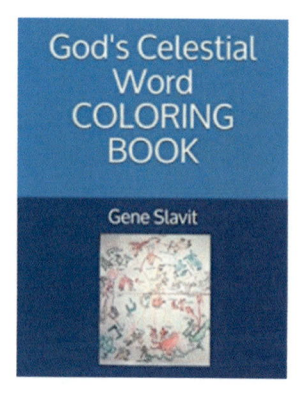

This companion to God's Celestial Word allows children to learn about the stars by coloring and learning in the 48 visible constellations. Includes star names and meanings.

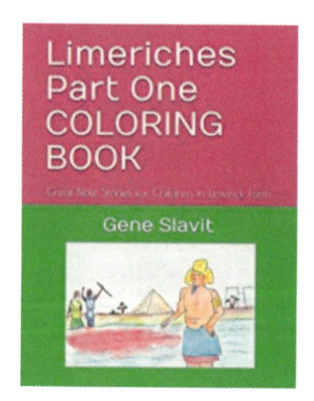

You can read your children limericks and let them color in great Bible stories. A companion coloring book to Limeriches Part One: Genesis to Job.

Let your child color the truths in *Aesop Revisited* for themselves!

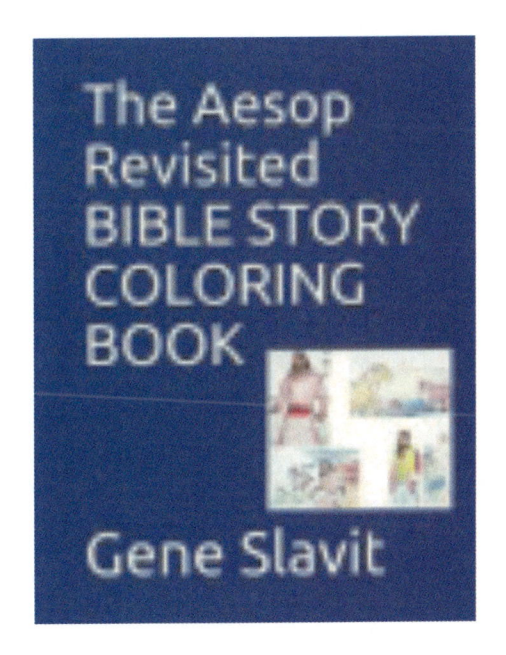

Only $4.99

Made in the USA
Middletown, DE
07 May 2021